I ESCAPED THE DONNER PARTY

PIONEERS ON THE OREGON TRAIL, 1846

ELLIE CROWE
SCOTT PETERS

I Escaped The Donner Part (I Escaped Book Five)

Copyright © 2020 by Ellie Crowe and Scott Peters

Library of Congress Control Number:

ISBN: 978-1-951019-13-6 (Hardcover)

ISBN: 978-1-951019-14-3 (Paperback)

While inspired by real events, this is a work of fiction and does not claim to be historically accurate or portray factual events or relationships. References to historical events, real persons, business establishments and real places are used fictitiously and may not be factually accurate, but rather fictionalized by the author.

Cover design by Susan Wyshynski

Best Day Books For Young Readers

I ESCAPED THE DONNER PARTY

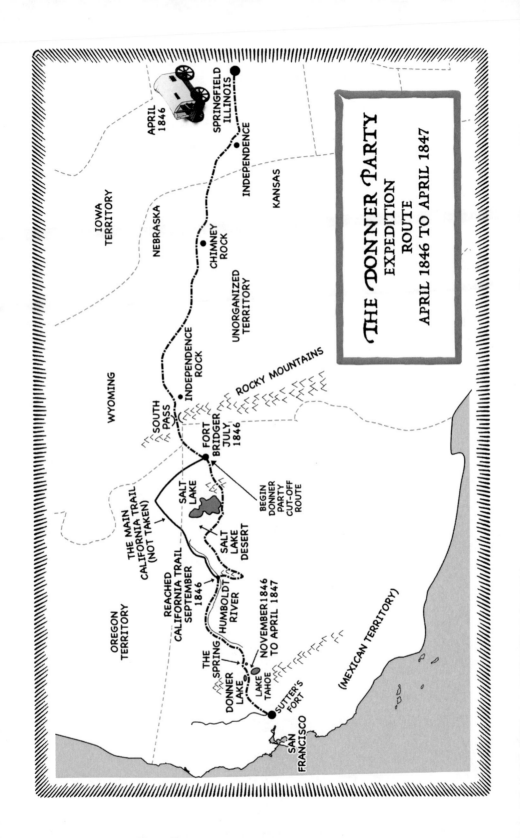

CHAPTER 1

Christmas 1846
Sierra Nevada Mountains
Nevada

The snowstorm thickened. Blinding. Icy.

With breaths coming in ragged gasps, fifteen-year-old Zeke stumbled through the whiteout. His friends, Lemuel and Mary Ann, were ominously silent. The only sounds were the howling wind, the howling wolves, and his own howling stomach.

Numb and exhausted, they were fourteen in all, the strongest members of the doomed Donner Party. Onward they struggled. To stop was to die.

Ahead, the Sierra Nevada summit lay in wait: a 7,200-foot-high mountain. A momentary break in the squall revealed jagged cliffs, looming like dizzyingly high prison walls.

Fat snowflakes fell.

Silent.

Merciless.

"We still have to climb that peak," Mary Ann croaked through dry lips. Her long dark hair hung in icicles. "Look at us, we can barely walk."

"We have to go on." Lemuel, a fifteen-year-old farm boy from Virginia, was tough as nails. Even on snowshoes, he tried to move with his usual swagger, but his eyes betrayed him.

Zeke knew Lemuel was afraid. And he was afraid too. Very afraid.

Mary Ann said, "What if it's a dead-end? Even the Indian guides are lost. What if we never get out of this terrible maze? What if we can't find our way forward or back?"

"Keep moving," Zeke said. "We've got to get to Sutter's Fort. We've got to bring help. If we don't, everyone back at Truckee Lake will starve."

The thought of all those little kids, children he knew well, made his chest hurt. More than sixty people had pinned their hopes on Zeke's party getting through the pass. Children and adults waited, starving to death, in makeshift, snow-covered cabins back at Truckee Lake.

Could he cross the Sierra Nevada and get help?

Maybe.

Maybe not.

Just keep putting one foot in front of the other. . .

Zeke trembled with hunger. His body warned him he was in danger. About to perish from starvation. He zoned out and snapped back to attention.

The temperature was plummeting. Darkness forced the party to stop. Zeke rummaged in his pack, found the flint, and managed to set fire to the top of a dead pine tree poking out of the snow. They all collapsed around the flames.

"Happy Christmas Eve," Zeke said and rubbed his belly. "Santa's reindeer would be a welcome sight."

Mary Ann shot him a smile that reminded him of better days. "Would you really eat Dasher and Dancer?" she said through blue lips.

"Yeah," Zeke said. "Yum, roast venison."

Foster, a family-leader, grunted. "We're all going to die unless we eat something real soon." His bushy hair jutted upward like boar-bristles.

An Irish teamster doubled over. "Won't be long before someone drops dead. When they do, the others should eat the body."

Zeke and Mary Ann exchanged nervous glances.

The burly Foster scanned the group. "Could be days before someone keels over. That'll be too late for us all. I say we draw sticks and eat the loser."

The group, as skinny as skeletons, stared at him with frightened eyes.

Horrified, Zeke shook his head. "No! We shouldn't do that."

"Keep quiet, you lunatic," Lemuel muttered. "Next thing, he'll eat you."

Cold clammy fear crept down Zeke's spine. From the hungry look in Foster's wolf-like eyes, he knew something terrible was going to happen. And it was going to happen soon.

With all his heart, he wished he'd never joined the Donner Party.

CHAPTER 2

June 1846
The Platte River
Nebraska
- Six months earlier -

Zeke's horse reared and he reined him in. "You're fine, Star Boy. What's got you spooked?"

Turning, he spotted a band of Indian braves watching from a grove of pines. Red and black war paint striped their faces. He sucked in his breath.

Word had it that the Pawnees, Sioux, and Snakes were warlike and merciless toward the whites. Every pioneer feared them.

The Indian braves studied Zeke but made no move to attack.

Fifteen-year-old Lemuel Murphy, a tough, fair-haired farm boy from Virginia, rode up on a black mule. "See the Indians?"

"Sure do." Zeke shook his horse's reins. "We're in Indian Territory. I guess they don't like having us here."

At least there was safety in numbers. Ahead, their wagon train snaked into the distance. And it was exciting—a once-in-a-lifetime adventure: a 2,000-mile trek from Illinois to California across prairies, deserts, and mountains. Hundreds of wagons were making the journey. He was one of seven teamsters driving the Reed family's oxen and caring for their cattle and saddle-horses.

Zeke's parents and brother had left Illinois a month earlier. Eventually, they'd reunite at Sutter's Fort in California. He was proud of his job. Best of all, he didn't have to travel in his family's wagon with his know-it-all big brother—or his father, the shape-up-or-ship-out General Farnsworth.

He watched the chain of wagons creaking along the muddy Oregon Trail. "Our boss's first wagon is huge," he said.

"You mean the Reed's Pioneer Palace Car?" Lemuel laughed. "It's two-story. They brought everything. Crazy! Big beds, chairs, there's even a wood cooking stove. Plus tools, books, and heaps of stuff to trade with Indians and Mexicans."

"That wagon must weigh a ton." Zeke frowned, watching the yoked oxen struggle to pull it. "The oxen are barely making two miles an hour. A toddler could walk to California faster."

"Hey, look!" Lemuel's eyes sparked up. "The families are nooning! Let's go!"

Zeke had learned that nooning meant eating lunch. And hard work had made him real hungry. Wind whipping his dark hair beneath his brimmed hat, he rode Star Boy to the shade trees.

Soon, plates loaded with pickled pork, baked beans, ham, bread, butter, cheese, dried fruit, and sugar jumble cookies were spread out on blankets on the grass. The Reed, Donner, Murphy, Breen, and Graves families and their teamsters sat and began scoffing down food.

"Dessert first!" Lemuel said.

"You got it!" Zeke grabbed two big sugar jumble cookies. This was the life. Here, he ate dessert first and no one cared. Back home, Pa made him eat his vegetables first, before even the meat.

He was glad he wasn't traveling with his family. Pa always got so mad so fast and threw punches when he'd been drinking —especially whenever Zeke had one of his visions.

Premonitions. Omens. Whatever the flashes of the future were, he hated them.

Once, he'd had a vision of Pa downing whiskey in a gentlemen's club, looking doomed as he stared at his hand of cards. Zeke had to stop the premonition from coming true. If Pa went to that club, he'd lose all his money. How could Zeke not warn him?

So he had.

Pa, furious, had called him crazy. His brother chimed in with *Zeke is a freak*. But when Zeke's warning proved right, Pa blamed him, said he caused it! Pa lashed out blindly, and that's how he lost his tooth.

Zeke's tongue found the gap between his teeth, glad it only showed when he grinned. He never told anyone Pa had knocked it out. And he definitely never told anyone about his weird flashes.

After it happened, he thought of running away. But his brother said no one would miss him, so he stayed.

In the end, Pa had to flee his creditors. That's why Zeke's family was headed for a new life in California. So, it wasn't all bad, because working on this wagon train was as good as running away. No one here knew about his weird flashes of the future. No one called him a freak.

And he intended to keep it that way.

CHAPTER 3

June 1846
The Platte River
Nebraska
- The Same Day -

A freckle-faced girl with wild red ringlets plopped down onto the blanket beside Zeke. "Hey Zeke, what are you planning to do when we get to California?"

Zeke smiled at Virginia Reed. She was his boss's daughter, thirteen years old, and she loved horses as much as he did.

"I'm going to breed racehorses," he said. "With stars on their foreheads. Just like Star Boy."

He'd seen it in a flash of his future, too; that had been one of his good flashes. He could still picture the green field and two ponies with their white stars. He sure hoped that flash came true.

"You'll find lots of good pastureland in California." Virginia grinned. "Papa read all about it in a book, *The Emigrants' Guide to Oregon and California.* The author, Lansford Hastings, has made this journey dozens of times."

Zeke listened with interest. "I'd love to see that book."

"Can't. Papa won't let us touch it." She pulled a face. "It's full of important maps and instructions."

"Like what?"

"Like start the journey in spring, and be sure to cross the Sierra Nevada Mountains before the first snowfall."

Zeke said, "Winter's not for ages."

"Exactly," Virginia said. "We're late, but Papa says not to worry."

Lemuel joined in. "I hope he knows how to handle the Indians. One of those braves waved a scalp at me. Not exactly friendly."

"He says that if the Indians attack, we've got to stand our ground," Virginia replied.

"Yeah, right!" Lemuel said. "I know what you'll do. You'll run for your life!"

Virginia gave him a long, hard stare. "You just wish you could ride as fast as me. Anyway, I bet the Indians wouldn't want yours—it would look like a monkey's scalp."

"Very funny," Lemuel said.

Virginia fell silent, staring out over the plains.

"What is it?" Zeke asked.

The wind tossed her red curls against her cheeks. "My great-aunt was captured by Indians."

"Did your family ever see her again?" Zeke asked.

Virginia's green eyes met his. "Not for five whole years. She escaped, but they say she was never the same."

Zeke and Lemuel digested this frightening news.

Virginia said, "When my mother heard we were traveling through Indian Territory, she cried for two days."

"We'd be safer if we could catch up to the big wagon train," Lemuel said. "But my pa says we've fallen hundreds of miles behind the others."

"Saddle up," James Reed shouted, a tin cup in one hand and a sandwich in the other. "And yoke my oxen, I want the two strong leaders pulling side-by-side. Enough eating and talking. Get a move on, Cecil."

Zeke winced at the sound of his given name. "Yes, sir." He sprang to his feet. James Reed was starting to sound real bossy. Just like Pa.

Lemuel snorted. "Get a move on, *Cecil!*"

Zeke glared. He hated being called Cecil. What if everyone began calling him that?

Lemuel had better watch it. Zeke would come up with a nickname for the teamster. One Lemuel wouldn't like. When teased, it was best to attack back fast. He'd learned that from having a mean older brother.

As they yoked the oxen, he worried about the hundreds of miles they'd fallen behind the larger wagon train. June or not, they were traveling too slow.

That's when the flash hit him.

He was stumbling through a world of ice. A white world. Cold. Deadly. The dark shadow of a man loomed over him. A huge man. A starving man. A predator prepared to kill.

The flash vanished.

Zeke took a shaky breath and found he was soaked with sweat.

Why on earth would a starving man, a predator, be after him?

That was the weirdest, scariest flash he'd ever had.

He sure hoped it didn't come true.

CHAPTER 4

25th June 1846
Chimney Rock, Nebraska

C himney Rock pointed skyward, towering in the pink dawn.

Zeke was on horseback, busy rounding up cattle. His horse had learned well. Star Boy was an expert at separating Reed's cows from the others.

"Well done, Star Boy," Zeke whispered. "You round 'em up like a cowboy's mount."

Star Boy was more than a horse—he was a friend and helper. Yesterday, they'd crossed the wide Platte River. There'd only been one way to do it: the hard way. They'd chopped logs, built rafts, and rolled the wagons aboard.

He'd never have managed without Star Boy. Their cattle and oxen, forced to swim alongside, had bellowed in fear. But his horse had stayed calm. Star Boy had even turned out to be a good swimmer.

Now Zeke urged the herd forward, but drew up when he spotted a board with a hand-painted warning:

Indians are hostile and dangerous. Killing and stealing stock. Arrows are tipped with rattlesnake venom.

Poison-tipped arrows? Zeke went on high alert.

This side of the Platte River belonged to the Sioux. The tribe had a scary reputation, and this confirmed it.

He clicked his tongue, anxious to get the herd moving. "I'm sure glad I have you with me, Star Boy."

Star Boy would gallop away from Indians fast as lightning.

He stiffened as Virginia came cantering up on her pony.

"The Sioux are on the warpath!" She was panting, her green eyes wide with fright. "Papa says bring the cattle close to the wagons. Hurry! The men are loading their rifles."

"Rifles?"

"Papa says we'll only fight if we have to."

"Right!" *Here we go!* Zeke clicked his tongue to Star Boy.

But before he and Virginia could speed the herd toward the wagons, five braves on skittering horses surrounded them. Red war paint streaked their sharp cheekbones. Tomahawks gleamed in their fists. Shrunken scalps dangled from their leather-strip necklaces.

Unsure what to do, Zeke raised his hand in greeting. He hoped it was a friendly greeting. He didn't feel friendly. His heart raced as he and Virginia eyed each other nervously. Here she'd come to warn him, and now they were stranded half-a-mile from the nearest wagon.

A brave held out two tanned buckskin robes. He pointed at Star Boy.

"No." Zeke shook his head, praying they wouldn't just kill him and take Star Boy anyway.

Another brave, offering a buffalo skin robe and beaded moccasins, pointed at Virginia's horse.

"No," Virginia tried to break free, prancing left and right. "We're not selling our horses. Zeke, let's go."

But they were trapped—the braves blocked them on all

sides. A sixth lean, hawk-nosed Indian came cantering up leading five ponies. He pointed at Virginia's horse. And then at Virginia herself.

What the heck? Hawk-nose wanted to trade the ponies for Virginia?

Virginia paled beneath her freckles, but her eyes flashed with fury.

"No!" Zeke spoke firmly and again shook his head.

Hawk-nose offered up a tattered soldier's coat.

Zeke swallowed, keenly aware these men were armed to the teeth. "No. I told you, no."

The brave pointed out the brass buttons as if they would clinch the sale. Grinning confidently, he reached out and gave Virginia's red ringlets a hard tug.

Virginia shrieked and her horse reared back. Zeke knew she was remembering her great-aunt who'd been taken by Indians. His heart slammed. These braves could easily kidnap his friend.

Hawk-nose grabbed hold of Virginia's horse's reins, and Zeke's hand flew to his knife. But what use would a small blade be against the tomahawks?

A loud Indian whoop made everyone turn.

A Sioux chief riding a big, black warhorse, fairly flew over the prairie. The chief waved a single-barreled shotgun. To Zeke's shock, he fired at his own braves.

Oh, brother! Zeke thought. Surely, he doesn't want to kill them!

The braves fled.

"Why did he do that?" Virginia's voice shook.

"No idea," Zeke said. "Let's go before he changes his mind."

Without another word, Zeke and Virginia bent low over their horse's manes and galloped to the closest wagon.

"Cecil!" Reed's voice rang out. "What are you doing? Corral the cattle!"

"But the—oh, never mind." He spun Star Boy around, glad to have the teamsters at his side as he doubled back.

They'd barely corralled the animals inside the circled wagons when hundreds of Sioux surrounded them, lining both sides of the trail. What now?

"Load your rifles," Reed shouted, tossing one to Zeke. "Show that you have them. Let them know we're ready to fight."

Zeke gripped his rifle hard.

But the braves came in peace. As the wagon train moved slowly on, the braves tossed green twigs at the pioneers.

When Zeke spotted the Sioux chief, he lifted his cowboy hat in thanks.

Virginia scowled at the braves. "They wanted to buy me."

Zeke nodded. "Yeah. Scary. I sure hope the Sioux stay friendly. They could wipe us out in seconds."

CHAPTER 5

July 1846
The Platte River, Wyoming
- One Month Later -

Sun-bleached buffalo skulls and bones littered the long sandbar that divided the river. People had scrawled messages on the eerie relics.

Zeke searched for a note from his parents and was disappointed to find none. Using a charcoaled stick, he wrote on a buffalo skull:

Zeke Farnsworth was here. We saw hundreds of Sioux. And we hunted buffaloes.

The buffalo hunt that morning had gone well until Sioux braves, riding high in their saddles, charged over the hill and caused a buffalo stampede.

He knew he shouldn't but he grinned just thinking about it:

the shaggy, stampeding animals, the thundering hooves, the whooping Sioux. Being a Sioux probably wouldn't be too bad!

"Hey, Cecil," Reed called out. "Wipe off that dumb grin and cut up those buffalo steaks!"

"Yeah, don't be a sloth, *Cecil*," Lemuel chuckled.

Virginia rode up. She'd missed the buffalo hunt when her ma made her scrub dirty clothes instead. She was clearly itching for her share of fun, because she shouted, "Who wants to race? I can outride you all!"

"I will!" Ten-year-old Edward Breen, freckled and skinny, swung himself into the saddle.

A vivid flash exploded in Zeke's mind. *Two galloping horses streaked across the sand. Without warning, one horse stumbled and fell. The rider flew over the horse's head. He crashed down and lay, lifeless.*

The image left Zeke seeing stars. He blinked, his throat dry.

He had to say something. But how could he warn his friends without giving himself away? It would start all over again, the taunts, the snubs, the wariness. Virginia and Edward would say he was weird. Soon, the rest of the pioneers would be saying it too.

What if they started muttering about witchcraft? He'd be in real danger.

But how could he not warn them?

"Virginia," he said. "Don't race out there. It's a bad spot."

"What?" She stared at him as if he was nutty as a squirrel.

"Just don't go, please."

"Why not?" she demanded.

Here we go. "Something might happen," he said. "Something bad."

She snorted. "Like what?"

"Someone might be thrown off a horse."

Virginia and Edward began to laugh.

"Why would you even say something like that?" she said. "As if we don't know how to ride?"

Zeke shrugged. He'd said as much as he was going to. Holding his breath, he watched Virginia and Edward gallop across the sand.

The disaster happened fast.

Edward's horse stumbled. The boy went flying.

Zeke raced to him.

Edward was pale with shock and pain and clutching his leg. "Pa is going to kill me," he moaned.

"Let me see." Zeke rolled up Edward's pant leg and winced. The boy's broken shinbone stuck right through his skin.

Why didn't they listen to me?

Virginia, pale and shaken, stared at Zeke with a strange look in her green eyes.

Edward's pa and ma ran up.

"Send for a surgeon," Edward's ma cried. "Send a rider

ahead to Fort Bridger, there'll be someone there. Please, God, hurry!"

As Edward's pa lifted him into their wagon, the boy fainted. His pa washed the wound. Then, looking as pale as his son, he clicked the bone back into place and bound the leg with a splint.

Hours passed before the barber-surgeon rode up on a mule. He carried a black bag bulging with tools and instruments. "I was trimming the captain's beard when I got your urgent message," he said. "Came as fast as I could. Where's my patient?"

The barber-surgeon gave Edward's broken leg one look and shook his head. "If that leg doesn't come off, it will kill him." He pulled out a wicked-looking saw. "We have to keep him still now." He turned to Zeke. "You, son, come and help hold down your friend."

Reluctantly, Zeke stepped forward.

'No, Pa," Edward moaned. "Don't let him. Don't let him saw off my leg, Pa."

"But son," his mother whispered. "He says it has to come off."

"Please, Ma." Edward's voice cracked. "Please, can we just leave my leg alone? Maybe it will heal, Ma. Maybe it will fix itself."

"Quick is best," the barber-surgeon muttered. He stroked his meat saw. "Three strokes and it's off."

Edward's pa cleared his throat. "We'll wait, sure we will," he said, his Irish accent soothing. "We'll give it a chance to heal."

"That's a fool's decision," the barber-surgeon huffed.

"We'll wait," Edward's pa said again.

An infected leg could get gangrenous, Zeke thought.

The barber-surgeon said, "You still have to pay me for my trouble. Whether I saw it off or not, I still get paid."

Zeke bent and spoke to his friend. "I'll pray for your leg to heal."

"I should have listened to you," Edward groaned.

His ma said, "Listened to him about what?"

Virginia shot Zeke a warning look.

"I just said the sandbank wasn't a good place to race," Zeke stammered.

To his relief, Reed strode up. "All done here?"

The barber-surgeon said, "Unfortunately, it seems so." He watched as Edward's parents rolled their wagon away from the gathered crowd. "However, I do have some good news for your party."

"And what's that?" Reed said.

Zeke edged closer as the barber-surgeon handed his boss an elegantly printed letter. "This is an open letter to all pioneers going to California. It's from Mr. Lansford Hastings, the famous travel guide."

"Lansford Hastings?" James Reed's face lit up as he began to read.

Lemuel and Virginia pressed close to Zeke's elbow. The three friends waited, breathless.

"It says he's discovered a shorter route to California," James Reed told the gathering crowd. "He calls it the Hastings Cut-off. If we want to take it, he'll meet us at Fort Bridger and be our guide. He says it's an easy road to Paradise."

Virginia whispered, "A shortcut? Papa will do that for sure. You know he reads Hastings' guidebook all the time."

A tiny woman with a surprisingly loud voice shouted, "Why take a different route? The route we're on is good and well-marked."

"Because the Hastings Cut-off is three hundred miles shorter," James Reed said.

Keeping her voice down so that only Zeke and Lemuel could hear, Virginia murmured, "I heard Papa talking to Ma. He's worried we're going too slow, we're way behind schedule. He wants to make sure we don't get stuck in the snow in the Sierra Nevada Mountains. This is good news."

Zeke felt a sliver of unease. He hoped taking the Hastings Cut-off wasn't a mistake.

It couldn't be. Could it?

Surely they could trust the advice of the well-known guide, Lansford Hastings?

CHAPTER 6

July - September 1846
The Hastings Cut-Off
Utah

Zeke stood at the fork in the road. He studied the countless wagon tracks on the famous trail leading north. The Hastings Cut-off, the unknown shortcut, led south. He'd been told that eventually, the trails would merge again on the far side of the Great Salt Lake. It was the 28th of July, and today the pioneers were making a very important decision.

"Papa says we're taking the Hastings Cut-off," Virginia said.

Zeke made a face. "The Oregon Trail, the one with lots of wagon wheel tracks, looks real good to me."

"The Hastings Cut-off is three-hundred miles shorter. It will save us time. The Murphy, Graves, Breen, and both Donner families are coming, too."

Zeke digested this news.

"The families elected George Donner as leader last night," Virginia said. "So we're called the Donner Party now. But they should have elected my papa, don't you think?"

Zeke felt uneasy. But it appeared he was the only one.

With only two days until August, the Donner Party split away from the large wagon train. In twenty creaking ox-wagons, the families set off south on the Hastings Cut-off. Excitement filled the air.

"Westward ho!" George Donner waved his bullwhip. "Forward to California!"

The pioneers cheered.

But almost immediately, things began to go wrong.

When they arrived at Fort Bridger, the man who'd promised to be their guide, Lansford Hastings, was nowhere to be found. Instead, he'd left a note at the barber-surgeon's trading store:

I've gone ahead with another pioneer group. Follow and catch up with me.

Catch up? How?

To make matters worse, the much-needed supplies offered at the barber-surgeon's trading store were way overpriced.

"I bet the barber-surgeon just lured us here to sell us stuff," Zeke told Lemuel.

Lemuel nodded. "How can we take this cut-off? We don't even have a map. My ma says we should go back and join the other wagons."

"Lansford Hastings left instructions," Virginia said. "Papa says we'll be fine."

Initially, the trail was easy and smooth. But to everyone's dismay, it soon became steep and slippery. After a backbreaking struggle, the pioneers reached Weber Canyon, where Lemuel spotted a note tacked on a sage bush.

"Uh oh," Lemuel said, scanning its contents. "It's from Hastings."

Zeke took it and read it with dismay:

Trail through canyon nearly impossible. Stay here. Wait for message.

"Come on," he said. "Let's show this to boss Reed."

Lemuel nodded.

"We'll have to turn around and go back to the fork," Zeke said.

But no. Instead, James Reed galloped ahead on his racing mare in search of Hastings. It took him four whole days to return. Zeke swallowed hard when Reed's saw his grim face. What was happening now?

"Hastings says he made a mistake. Weber Canyon is a nightmare for wagons," Reed said. "The group he's leading barely made it through. He says winter is coming and he doesn't have time to come back for us. He sends his regrets."

Lemuel snorted, "Sends his regrets!"

"I told you, we should turn back," Zeke said.

Reed overheard and his frosty blue eyes flashed. "There's no time to turn back, Cecil, we're already dangerously late. Hastings told me about an alternate route through the Wasatch Mountains. We'll take that."

"No one wants your advice, *Cecil*," Lemuel whispered with a grin.

"Watch it, *Mule*," Zeke said.

With no trail whatsoever, they set off through Utah's steep Wasatch Mountains.

"So much for the *easy road to Paradise*," Zeke said. "It's impossible for the oxen to pull the wagons."

"We'll have to clear a wagon trail," Reed said. "Starting now."

"I know, sir." A sense of foreboding lit a fire under Zeke as he got down to work.

Day after day, the men hacked trees and moved boulders. They inched forward at a painfully slow rate. Water was growing scarce, and cattle stumbled and fell on the rocky ground. The effort drained the pioneers and animals. Zeke was devastated when Virginia's beloved pony collapsed and refused to move.

After more than three weeks, the eighty pioneers stumbled out of the mountains.

Winter is coming fast, Zeke thought. Already, leaves were turning crimson and gold. From the broad mountain slope, he stared down at the next disaster—the Great Salt Lake.

It looked even worse than it sounded. Mile upon mile of glistening white salt made him lick his lips in thirst. Beyond the eerie, salty shores lay the wastelands of the Forty Mile Desert.

This wagon trail was the pits. Lansford Hastings was out of his mind to recommend it.

The pioneers descended and found a freshwater spring just before the Salt Lake. A message from Hastings warned of things to come:

Hard travel two days and two nights across desert. No water or grass.

"Hastings must be returning on horseback to leave these messages," Virginia said. "I guess he's worried about us, but I wish we never followed his advice. And his group doesn't have cattle herds like we do."

Zeke studied the desert and shook his head. "How will the herds ever get across this?"

"We don't have a choice," Reed said, his voice flat. "We'll fill buckets with water and grass and make a run for it. We'll travel day and night. No stopping."

Day after day, the sun burned down. The salt crust broke under the heavy wagons, and the wagon wheels sank into quicksand.

"Gee haw!" Zeke cracked his bullwhip. "Move!"

But the weary oxen didn't feel like moving.

CHAPTER 7

July - September 1846
The Hastings Cut-Off
Utah

By the fourth day, they'd run out of water. The miserable, thirsty animals bellowed.

"Here you are," Zeke murmured. He wiped the animals' tongues with a wet rag and shared his water canteen with Star Boy. But he knew it wasn't enough.

Animals lay down on the burning salt and refused to get up. On the fifth day, nine cattle dropped dead.

Star Boy looked at Zeke with trusting, brown eyes.

"I should never have brought you on this crazy journey, Star Boy," he whispered.

Reed scanned the cloudless sky. "I'll ride ahead and see how far it is to a spring. Make sure you take proper care of my herd, Cecil."

Zeke scowled. "Yeah, right." Reed's decision to take the

Hastings Cut-off had endangered them all. "Reed drives me crazy," he muttered to Lemuel.

"You and me both, brother," Lemuel said. "He thinks we're just stupid kids."

"Reminds me of my Pa," Zeke said.

They were watching the dark desert for Indians when Reed came galloping back.

"I found springs!" Reed shouted. "Freshwater springs! About twenty miles from here."

Zeke's heart leapt. "Great news, sir!"

"Unyoke the oxen and drive them and the cattle there. We'll water them well. Then we'll bring the oxen back to fetch the wagons. Mind you keep the herd together, Cecil," Reed warned.

"Yes, sir," Zeke grunted.

It would be nice if Reed trusted him to do his job by now without calling him out—he'd been working his butt off keeping the herd together for months.

Reed rode away to the wagons to tell his wife the good news.

Zeke and the teamsters set to work. But things went terribly wrong, fast. The minute they'd freed the herds, the animals charged into the dark desert.

"They smell the water," Zeke shouted. "After them!"

But the cattle and oxen had disappeared.

"Reed's going to kill us," Zeke groaned. "His whole herd is gone. You guys go ahead and search for them. I'll let him know."

On hearing the news, Reed let out a roar.

Zeke felt awfully guilty.

"Those cows charged off like bats out of hell," he told Lemuel.

"Reed's roar would have made a mad bull proud," Lemuel muttered.

"Can't say I blame him," Zeke said. "His whole herd has gone! And how's he going to pull his four wagons?"

Reed called out, "Cecil! Help Mrs. Reed with the children. We've hardly any water left. We'll all have to walk to the springs tonight. Hopefully, we'll find the herd there."

"It's twenty miles to the springs," Virginia gasped.

With Mrs. Reed and four-year-old Tommy propped on his horse, the boss marched off in the springs' direction.

Zeke lifted Virginia's eight-year-old sister, Patty, and little brother, Jimmy, onto Star Boy's saddle. He and Virginia walked beside them while Zeke lugged the last small bucket of water.

Five-year-old Jimmy wiggled around and stared at Patty. "You've got your dolly in your apron pocket," he said. "Pa will be mad, he said no toys."

"Dolly is not a toy." Patty pouted defiantly.

Zeke grinned. So there was a Reed family rebellion going on. Even angelic-looking Patty was tired of being bossed around. He looked ahead to see if Reed had heard, but the rest of the family didn't turn around.

As a bright moon rose over the shimmering white salt lake, he heard a strange sound—spooky music.

"What the heck's that?" he said.

Virginia listened wide-eyed. "Spirits? Ghosts?"

"It sounds like a piano," Zeke said. "Who could be playing a piano?"

"Oh," Virginia gave a hollow laugh. "I know what it is. It's my music teacher's piano. I guess his wagon was too heavy for the oxen to pull and he's had to leave the piano behind. The wind will play it now."

"Or the Indians." Zeke looked into the night.

The desert was filled with unexpected shapes: a rocking chair rocked to-and-fro; a cactus wore a leather hat. To lighten their wagons, pioneers had clearly abandoned things as they went.

Earlier, he and Reed had dug a deep hole to bury pots, pans, and clothing. *The Indians will find it all the minute we're gone,* he thought.

The wind rose. Sharp granules struck Zeke's face. Soon even his eyelashes were coated with sand and salt. He longed to tip up the bucket and take a drink, but it was all they had.

A wagon creaked to a halt behind them, driven by someone who'd had the wits to keep his oxen from running off. Zeke turned to see a dark shape leap down and stomp across the sand toward them. As he drew closer, Zeke recognized Snyder, a frontiersman with the arms of a weightlifter. Then he saw the rifle. Big, black, and pointed at his chest.

He inhaled sharply. *What now? Is Snyder the dangerous man I saw in that flash? Is this desert the white world I saw?*

"Give me that water," Snyder demanded.

"I can't give it to you," Zeke said. "It's all we have."

"You lie," Snyder said. "I know you have more. Give it to me. Now!"

"Sorry, no," Zeke said. "You can get water yourself when we reach the springs."

"I want that bucket now." Snyder cocked the rifle.

Virginia pulled at the bucket handle. "Give it to him."

Reluctantly, Zeke handed it over.

"Not worth dying over," Virginia muttered.

Eyes narrowed in anger, Zeke watched Snyder stroll off swinging the bucket. "If he didn't have the rifle, I'd grab the bucket from the maniac and wallop him over the head."

The flash came fast. He saw Snyder lying facedown on the desert sand, motionless and covered with blood.

"Oh, brother!" he gasped. "I wanted to knock Snyder out, not kill him." He rubbed his eyes hard.

"What? Zeke! What's wrong?" Virginia grabbed his arm.

Little Jimmy stared at Zeke. "What's the matter, Zeke?"

"Nothing," Zeke shook his head. "Nothing."

The flashes were getting worse.

CHAPTER 8

Early September 1846
Pilot Peak Foothills
Nevada

Dawn came quickly. As green patches appeared in the distance, Zeke began to run. The spring! Lots of springs! Wonderful, bubbling water.

Hungry animals tore at the grass and thirsty people gulped down water. But there was no sign of Reed's herd.

"Dang," Zeke muttered. "I sure hope the Indians didn't take the herd."

"Maybe Papa found them already," Virginia said. She ran off with Patty and Jimmy to find their parents. Zeke took a few enormous gulps of cool water and burped loudly.

He let Star Boy drink his fill and then hopped into the saddle. He needed to find that herd, fast.

Rounding a clump of palms, he bumped into Lemuel.

"Pretty much a disaster, huh?" Lemuel said.

"Yeah. It's bad." As one of the teamsters in charge of the animals, Zeke knew he was partly to blame. Not only did he feel guilty, he knew Reed wouldn't let him forget it.

Lemuel winced. "Ours smelled the water and charged off too. I bet the Indians have them."

"I sure hope not."

"Hey, Cecil," Lemuel said. "There's not much we can do now."

"If the leaders are smart, they'll order a search party."

They sat in glum silence for a long time.

Finally, Lemuel jabbed him with an elbow. "You stink. "

"Speak for yourself, Mule," Zeke said and sniffed at his armpit. He did stink.

Lemuel grinned. "How about a dip? At least we can get this desert off our backs."

They pulled off their sweaty clothes and jumped into the inviting spring. The cold water felt great on his sore limbs and weather-beaten skin.

Edward Breen ran up and leaped into the pool.

Zeke stared at the 10-year-old in surprise. "Hey Ed, your leg looks fine!"

"Yeah! It fixed itself." Edward grinned. "Me and Pa have watered and fed all our cattle already."

"You're lucky," Lemuel said. "My pa's talked to lots of people. More than one hundred animals have died or are missing."

Zeke groaned. If they couldn't find the cattle, they'd be in huge trouble. Without the oxen, they couldn't pull the wagons. And without the cows, they'd have no meat or milk.

Soon, a new search party was organized. Zeke spent the morning on horseback, searching desperately. Twice, arrows whistled past Zeke's ears. Indians, he thought.

"You lose any animals?" he called out to Mary Ann.

"Our cattle and oxen died in the desert." Mary Ann's big eyes brimmed with tears. "We can't move our wagon without oxen. Pa says we'll have to walk."

"Walk!" Zeke swallowed hard. Mary Ann had eight young brothers and sisters. How could they carry enough food and blankets? Their wagon was their home away from home. A place to shelter from the elements. How would they survive without it?

Zeke wished he could help, but the mountains lay ahead and he'd be lugging what he could of the Reeds' belongings. With just two animals, his boss was reduced to only one wagon.

"Maybe Mr. Reed will let one of two of your toddlers ride in his wagon. Try asking Mrs. Reed."

"Okay. Thank you." Mary Ann nodded.

Keseberg, a giant of a man with a dirty blond beard, joined them. "I've lost one of my wagons too," he growled, studying them through hooded eyes. "It's Reed's fault." He ran his hand over Star Boy's rump. "Your horse doesn't look too good. Let me know when you decide to eat him. I'll buy a chunk." He licked his lips with his fat, red tongue. "Horse meat is good."

"Are you crazy? I'm never doing that!" Zeke covered Star Boys' twitching ears just in case he somehow understood. How dare Keseberg?

"That man's creepy," Mary Ann whispered. "Two days ago, he left a crippled man from his party behind in the desert. Keseberg said he was too heavy for the wagon."

Zeke stared after Keseberg in horror. "That's barbaric."

"They're desperate. They're turning against one another," Mary Ann said. "I wish we were back home."

At noon, Reed called a meeting. "We're low on provisions and there's more than seven-hundred miles to go. I need volunteers to ride ahead to Sutter's Fort for supplies. Two men on horseback should be able to get there fast. Once Captain Sutter hears our problems, I'm sure he'll send food and mules."

"I'll go!" Zeke yelled. "Me and Star Boy will be over the Sierra Nevada in no time."

I'd love to leave this mess, he thought. California, here I come!

"You're here to take care of my herd, not go running off," Reed said. "And you'd better find them, Cecil."

Zeke nodded. "My name is *Zeke*," he muttered under his breath.

Two men were chosen and Zeke watched them leave. Far in the distance, he could see dark clouds covering the scary-high peaks of the Sierra Nevada. That morning he'd seen geese flying south.

Winter was coming.

He shivered.

Oh, brother. I hope those fat clouds aren't filled with snow.

CHAPTER 9

Late September 1846
The Humboldt River, Nevada

Zeke was worried, so worried about Star Boy. That morning, the first snow dusted the tops of the surrounding hills. What if snow filled the mountain pass ahead? His horse was thin and weak and would quickly die trying to struggle through deep snow.

Reed was away from camp when two Paiute Indians approached their wagon. With enthusiastic signs, they told Zeke and Mrs. Reed they'd seen cattle in the desert.

"I don't trust any of them," Mrs. Reed muttered. She motioned to the Indians to go.

But the young braves looked friendly and their horses were well fed and healthy. Although many Indians had stolen or killed the pioneers' cattle, it seemed these two wanted to help.

Zeke made up his mind fast. If he was going to do this, it had to be now. He rode after the Paiute and called out to them to stop. As they reined in their horses, he slid out of the saddle.

Star Boy looked at him with dark, trusting eyes.

"I should never have brought you on this crazy journey, Star Boy," he whispered.

Then, swallowing hard, Zeke handed Star Boy's reins to the closest brave.

The brave looked confused.

"Please take care of my horse," Zeke said. "His name is Star Boy." Then, choking up and unable to talk, he simply pointed to his heart and then to Star Boy.

Solemnly, the brave nodded.

Zeke wrapped his arms around Star Boy's pitifully bony neck. "I love you," he whispered. "Really love you. May God protect you."

Star Boy gave him a puzzled where-am-I-going-and-what-are-you-doing-look.

Heart breaking, Zeke turned away.

Within minutes, the braves and Star Boy were gone. Deal with it, Zeke told himself. Star Boy has a better chance of surviving now.

On September 26, a miracle happened. They spotted old wagon wheel tracks marking the trail. At long last, the Hastings Cut-off route had rejoined the well-known route to California.

"I could lie down and kiss those wagon wheel tracks," Virginia said. "All those families we started off with passed by here."

"They're probably in California already." Zeke pictured his family safe and sound and enjoying the sunshine.

"Yes, but it's not my papa's fault," Virginia muttered. "Blame Lansford Hastings."

"I know." Zeke scanned the frowning faces surrounding him.

The pioneers all wished they'd stayed with the other wagon train. They blamed Reed.

Filled with anxiety, they hardly talked to one another anymore.

As Zeke drove two reluctant cows up a sandy riverbank, he heard shouting.

"Hey! Mule!" Zeke called. "What's going on?"

Lemuel grinned. "I don't know, but I feel left out!"

"Me too!" Zeke said. "Let's go see."

It was Reed and Snyder.

"Stop whipping those oxen," Reed roared. "You trying to kill them?"

Snyder shouted back. "You gonna tell me how to drive my oxen?" He cracked his bullwhip at the pitiful beasts.

"Stop, now!" Reed yelled.

"You gonna make me?" Snyder cracked his bullwhip again.

Zeke said, "Looks like Reed is bossing around someone else."

"Reed versus Snyder! Sounds like a fight," Lemuel said. "That'll be worth seeing."

"Yeah, well, Snyder's a creep. He stole our last bucket of water," Zeke said. "I hope Reed demolishes him."

Reed's voice rang out. "We'll settle this later."

"We'll settle it now!" Snyder snarled.

"Wait till we get up the slope." Reed sounded impatient. Even bored.

Snyder's face went red with fury. "No. Now."

Zeke said, "Hey, Mule. If it's a fistfight, ten cents Reed wins."

Lemuel gave him a thumbs-up. "You're on, Cecil!"

Snyder moved fast. He smashed the heavy butt-end of his bullwhip down on Reed's head. Reed staggered, and before he could recover, Snyder struck him again. And then a third time.

"No!" Zeke shouted, running forward. *Snyder's going to kill Reed. He must be the dangerous man I saw in the flash!*

With a scream, Mrs. Reed darted between the two men to stop the fight. Snyder's bullwhip struck her. She screamed and clutched her bleeding shoulder.

Bellowing in rage, Reed drew his hunting knife and lunged. Like a knife going into butter, the hunting knife slid through Snyder's jacket. Snyder clutched the hilt with both hands. Then, he fell to the ground.

Zeke froze in horror.

"What have I done?" Reed stammered.

Zeke and Mr. Breen ran to Snyder and tried to stem the blood. They couldn't. No one could. In fifteen minutes, Snyder was dead.

Zeke stared at his blood-slicked hands. What had happened

was unbelievable. Snyder, a solid frontiersman a few minutes ago, lay motionless.

Just like in Zeke's flash.

"I didn't mean to do it," Reed gasped. "What have I done?"

"Murder!" Keseberg shouted. "Murder! That's what you've done!" He turned to the excited crowd. "I say hang Reed," he shouted. "An eye for an eye. That's justice."

No! Surely they wouldn't hang Reed? From the look of the flushed, angry faces, Zeke could see that some people would. Snyder, the dead frontiersman, had been a popular man, strong and lively.

Unfortunately, Reed wasn't exactly Mr. Popularity. As for Keseberg, the creepy bearded man who'd wanted to eat Star Boy had gathered a number of supporters.

"Lynch him! Lynch him!" Keseberg chanted.

Two others joined in.

"Someone has to stop this," Zeke muttered.

Lemuel rolled his eyes. "Feeling suicidal, Cecil?"

Zeke took a deep breath and stepped forward. He looked directly at Mr. Breen. "Sir, I saw Mr. Snyder pound Mr. Reed with the bullwhip. He whipped Mrs. Reed too. Mr. Reed was defending his wife."

Keseberg growled. "I'll get the rope. You can hang him from my wagon plank "

A few shouted their approval.

Mr. Breen drew his pistol. "Stand down, you idiots. We'll let the law in Sutter's Fort decide. This sounds to me like self-defense."

"I didn't mean to kill him," Reed shouted. "It was an accident."

Someone called out, "He thinks he's above the law!"

A hasty trial was called. Mr. Breen huddled with the other

family leaders, talking low and earnestly. Finally, he called for attention.

"It's been decided. James Reed will be banished."

Zeke gaped. They were sending his boss off to fend for himself in the desert?

Keseberg roared, "Hang the monster! Hang 'im!"

Virginia started screaming. "Leave my papa alone."

"Reed will be banished," Mr. Breen repeated.

Mrs. Reed clutched her husband's arm. "Take the horse, James. Please. Take it. And go."

Reed shook his head. "I can't take it and leave you and the children without it, Margaret. How could you possibly manage?"

"Ride to Sutter's Fort, my love." Tears ran down Mrs. Reed's cheeks. "When you return with supplies from Captain Sutter, they'll forgive you and welcome you back."

"Hang him!" Keseberg yelled. "He'll look well hanging from a rope."

Mr. Breen moved in front of him. "No hanging," he said firmly.

"All right, send him off. But no horse," Keseberg said. "No weapons. No food."

"Sending a man out into the wilderness with no horse, weapons, or food is as good as hanging him," Zeke said hotly.

"Please let my papa take his horse," Virginia begged.

After more discussion, it was agreed. Reed could take his horse but nothing else.

Looking stunned, Reed hugged his wife and children.

Virginia, sobbing, watched her father ride away. Then she turned to Zeke. "Meet me after supper," she whispered.

That night, Virginia and Zeke snuck away to a stand of boulders where Reed was waiting. Virginia handed her father his rifle, ammunition, a hunting knife, and a bag of hard biscuits and dried beef strips. She hugged him for a long time.

Reed shook Zeke's hand. "Take care of my family, Cecil. My wife will need your help."

When Zeke looked into Reed's eyes, he saw trust. And respect. Had that been there all along? Had he been blinded by his own insecurities?

Zeke nodded. "Yes, sir, I will."

He vowed he'd do everything he could to deserve Reed's trust.

Reed and his gray mare disappeared into the dark night.

This is bad, Zeke thought. We've got more than six hundred miles to go until we reach Sutter's Fort. And now we've lost one of the most experienced leaders.

What's next?

CHAPTER 10

Late October 1846
Near present day Reno, Nevada
- Three weeks later -

Z eke pulled five-year-old Jimmy Reed up the steep
incline. "Almost there," he lied.

The exhausted pioneers had crossed the Forty Mile
Desert. Now they faced one last hurdle—the worst one—the
towering Sierra Nevada mountains.

"One last push over the mountains," he told Jimmy. "You've
trekked two thousand miles already. You're a champ. You can
do it."

Jimmy shook his head. "I don't want to climb those big
mountains."

"See the circle around the moon," Edward warned. "Pa says
that means a storm's coming."

Zeke tried to laugh. It came out as a gulp. "That's just an
Irish superstition."

"Maybe not," Edward said.

Something buzzed past Zeke's ear. Arrows!

What the heck! Indians!

Ducking, he spun to see them holed up in a clump of pines, firing arrow after arrow at the remaining animals.

Zeke grabbed the rifle and returned fire. Other pioneers joined him, shooting furiously. But by the time the Indians left, nineteen oxen and cattle had been wounded or killed.

More wagons had to be abandoned. Reluctantly, food and goods were left behind. Some travelers struggled onward on foot, weighed down with toddlers and supplies. Others drove the remaining frightened animals toward a slippery thousand-foot granite slope.

Zeke shook his head. There was no way the Reed's one ox and one cow could haul their remaining wagon up the steep rise.

He went to speak with Mrs. Reed. "We'll have to leave the wagon here, ma'am. We'll have to go on without it."

Mrs. Reed took a rasping breath and nodded. "But I have to rest, son. I can't walk another step."

As Zeke gathered fire kindling, he started in shock.

Three men riding mules were descending the slope. Squinting through the fog, he recognized Charles Stanton. These were the volunteers who'd gone to Sutter's Fort for help; they'd made it! They were towing four pack mules strapped with bulging sacks.

"Mr. Stanton! You brought supplies!" he yelled.

"I did." Although he looked exhausted, Stanton smiled. "Even better, I brought two Miwok Indian guides! They led me through the pass and they'll lead us all back to California. Mountain men at the fort say we've at least a full month before the big winter snowstorms hit."

"That's great news," Zeke said.

As excited pioneers swarmed around him, Stanton unstrapped the sacks. Eager hands reached for the biscuits and dried beef.

He turned to Margaret Reed. "I saw your husband.

Margaret Reed's face lit up. "My husband is alive!"

"He's at Sutter's Fort gathering a relief party. It's taking a while because California is at war with Mexico, and most men are fighting."

She turned to her four children, "We must stay strong. Virginia, Patty, can you do it?"

The two girls nodded eagerly.

"Papa is alive!" Virginia murmured a prayer of thanks.

"Let's go!"

With the small children on Stanton's mules, they continued on up the slippery granite. The trail headed to the sky, growing steeper by the minute. They passed a family who had removed the wheels from their wagon, turning it into a sort of sled, but the cattle weren't having much luck trying to drag it.

They soon caught up with the Graves, Murphy, and Foster families, all of whom were now wagon-less. Lemuel, Billy, and Mary Ann labored to drive the oxen. The beasts, loaded with goods and young children, bellowed rebelliously. Some simply braced their legs and refused to move.

"Hey, Mule!" Zeke shouted. "Your oxen are as stubborn as you are. Want some bread? Stanton brought supplies!"

Lemuel grabbed a chunk and inhaled deeply. "Smells good!" He broke off a piece for ten-year-old Billy. "We haven't had bread for ages."

Then, just as things seemed to be improving, feathery snowflakes began to fall.

Zeke closed his eyes in despair.

Snow.

The dreaded snow.

CHAPTER 11

31st October 1846
The Sierra Nevada Mountains

At first, the snow was soft. Pretty.

The little Reed boys laughed and licked their cracked lips. In the whirling flakes, the mountain peak looming over them was beautiful, like a giant turreted castle.

"I'll ride ahead to make sure the pass is still open," Stanton said.

Following the two Indian guides, he disappeared into the white haze.

The pioneers huddled together in the swirling snow. Shivering children clung to their parents while toddlers howled.

Zeke found a dry pine tree and set it alight. The warmth felt good. People spread oxhides over the snow, then settled on them to wait. With a blanket over his head, Zeke lay listening to the night. Cattle moaned, the wind wailed, and wolves howled at the moon.

Suddenly, he heard Stanton's excited voice.

"The pass is open! Hurry! We can still get through if we keep right on."

"Yes!" Zeke ripped off his blanket and jumped to his feet.

Mrs. Reed stood, swayed, and almost fell. "We can't possibly cross the summit now," she said. "It's pitch dark. The children are exhausted. Let's just rest a few hours. We'll go at first light."

"Let's go now," Zeke said. "We can do it."

Mr. Breen spoke. "No. It would be madness to go in the dark. We'd lose the cattle down a gorge. Or break our legs. No, we'll wait till first light."

Stanton nodded reluctantly, but Zeke saw the Miwok Indians exchange glances. The Miwok knew what they were doing. A sense of foreboding ran through him.

All night, the wild wind howled and screeched—a triumphant banshee. A small voice urged Zeke to walk onward alone. I can get over the mountains, he thought. If I leave right now, I could be in California tomorrow.

Do it, he told himself.

Just get up and go.

Snow fell, mixed with pelting hailstones.

Four-year-old Tommy Reed began to cry, plaintive sobs calling for his papa. Five-year-old Jimmy, shivering and damp, buried his head on Zeke's leg.

Zeke longed to go.

But how could he?

Snow fell in larger and larger flakes. The blanket covering him grew wet and heavy.

At dawn, he peeked out. The world was white. Everything—

the people, the cattle, the oxen—had disappeared. All he saw was snow.

Had they left without him?

For a moment, he panicked. "Hey!" he shouted. "Hey! Is anyone there?"

Heads popped out of the drifts. Cattle and mules floundered beneath snowbanks, only their noses and the tops of their heads visible.

Stanton struggled upright until he stood unsteadily. "Come on, everyone up. Only three miles to the pass."

This was it! They were on their way.

Zeke grabbed hold of Jimmy's hand. "We can do it!"

"Yeah!" little Jimmy cheered. "And we'll see Papa soon!"

Faces tense, people dug themselves and their children free of the drifts.

Lemuel stared at the white world. "I never saw snow so bad before. How many feet do you think?"

Zeke shook his head. "Some of those drifts must be thirty feet."

"The animals can't move," Lemuel groaned. "We'll have to leave them."

A flurry of snow blinded Zeke. "Let's go!" He pulled Jimmy along. Jimmy was a stoic little guy and doing his best, but some steps sank him chest-deep.

Higher they trekked until the trail narrowed, teetering above an impossibly deep crevasse. The group inched along the ridge, where falling meant death in the yawning abyss below.

"Are we nearly there?" little Jimmy asked.

"Yes. Nearly." Zeke had no idea. He couldn't even see the summit through the falling snow.

"One mile from the summit!" Stanton shouted. "Only one more mile!"

But it was too late.

The narrow mountain pass, with grim crags looming on either side, was totally blocked by snow.

It was utterly impossible to go further.

Zeke's chest tightened. Last night, they could have got through.

Last night they had a chance.

They'd made a horrible mistake.

CHAPTER 12

November 1846
Truckee Lake (Now called Donner Lake)
Eastern Slopes of the Sierra Nevada
- Temperature 22 degrees below zero -

Huddled on the high, narrow ridge, Zeke scanned the black, threatening clouds.

"Storm's getting worse," he said.

Barely visible in the gale stood Mrs. Reed, head bent and silent.

Zeke inched along until he found Stanton. "There's an old cabin back at the lake."

Stanton nodded. "I saw it too. We'll turn around and set up camp, wait for the snow to melt and try again."

Faces grim, the pioneers stumbled mile after mile back down the mountain. Truckee Lake's waters, blue just two days ago, were now black and frozen. Snow blanketed everything.

Virginia shivered. "We can't all fit in that cabin. There're nearly eighty people. We'll freeze to death out here. What do you think the temperature is?"

Zeke shook his head. "Someone said twenty-two below zero. Take the little kids to the cabin."

Pulling her wet blanket around her shoulders, Virginia nodded and herded dozens of children inside.

Zeke grabbed an ax. She was right. Without shelter, they'd die.

For hours, the pioneers chopped down pines and hewed logs. By late afternoon, they'd managed to construct four rough log shacks for the families. They still needed roofs, though, so they slaughtered cattle, skinned them, and stretched the rawhides overhead. Lean-tos were added, propped against walls and boulders.

Last, the exhausted crew hacked up the slaughtered cattle and covered the meat with snow.

Darkness came early. Zeke and Virginia ferried supplies from the wagon into the Reed's half of a log cabin. A rawhide curtain divided their half from Mary Ann's family. Through it,

Mary Ann could be heard trying to get her eight little brothers and sisters dry and fed.

As the storm intensified, Virginia made a small fire in the center of the room. Soon, a pot of melted snow bubbled with chunks of beef.

Her mother motioned to Zeke. "Come join us."

"That would be great!" Thankful to be invited, Zeke sat and inhaled deeply. "Smells good."

"I'm glad we have a fire," Jimmy said. "This is a big adventure."

"Sure is." Zeke ate a mouthful of stew and licked his lips. "At least we aren't out in that raging storm. What a place!"

"We'll leave as soon as the snow stops," Virginia said.

"Hope so." Zeke nodded. From the sound of the screeching blizzard, they weren't going anywhere soon. He curled up in his damp blanket and fell into an exhausted sleep.

By morning, he was hungry and ready to go a-hunting. The snow had half-buried the cabin, and he had to dig his way out. While the snow had stopped, winds sent flurries gusting into his face. Rifle in hand, he stomped to the frozen lake.

Lemuel and his ten-year-old brother, Billy, were already there.

"Get anything?" Zeke asked.

"Not even a rabbit," Lemuel said. "No grass here, so no game. The animals must be down in the lower valleys."

"I bet there're fish in the lake." Zeke pictured fresh trout crisping on a fire, and his stomach rumbled. Dark shapes moved under the ice. Fish! No matter what, he'd catch one.

He broke a hole in the frozen lake, and they spent the afternoon bobbing lines up and down. No fish took the bait.

"You're not much good at fishing, Cecil," Lemuel said.

"Get lost, Mule! I'm about as good as you are at hunting."

"You don't have to be mean," Lemuel muttered.

But Zeke was too worried to answer. He surveyed the frozen lake and desolate mountains. He'd seen a snowy place just like this in that awful flash: *The icy world of white. The dangerous, starving man, a predator with menacing eyes. Coming for him.*

Zeke had the eerie feeling that this was the place.

CHAPTER 13

December 1846
Truckee Lake (Now called Donner Lake)
Eastern Slopes of the Sierra Nevada

D ays turned into weeks. Storm followed storm—
shrieking whiteouts that buried their cabins deeper
and deeper.

The pioneers ate the last of their wagon supplies. Then, they
ate the meat buried in the snow. With no game and no fish,
meals dwindled to scraps.

"Mama says if we can't find food," Virginia said. "We'll have
to eat poor little Cash."

Zeke looked at the small, thin dog. "What about mice?" he
said. "I heard some scampering around."

She nodded. So that night, they lay in wait. Cash joined
them, tail wagging. At the first squeak, Zeke leaped up with a
hammer in hand. *Bang!*

"Got one!" he whispered.

They fell silent, listening. It took nearly all night, but they managed to catch two more. It felt like a miracle.

That day, they chewed their way through mouse stew. Cash munched on mouse tails and feet.

Forty more long, hungry days passed. By now, snow reached the cabin roof and covered the tops of the pines. It was impossible to get dry wood for the fire. Zeke and Virginia chipped away at the log walls. Day and night they huddled together, cold and starving. Two-year-old Tommy lay on his stomach, chewing the rawhide rug.

Face thin and strained, Mrs. Reed pulled one of the rawhides off the roof. They removed the hair, scrubbed it, cut it into strips, and boiled it.

"It tastes disgusting!" Patty shuddered.

"Not that bad. Eat it!" Zeke gulped down the gluey soup. He knew some of the other teamsters were literally starving.

As hide after hide was used for soup, snow began to trickle into the cabin.

"We have to stop stripping the roof," Mrs. Reed said.

Virginia looked pointedly at Zeke's leather riding boots, protruding from his canvas sack of belongings.

Zeke followed her glance. His ma had given him those boots for his fifteenth birthday and he loved them. They reached almost to his knees, with special heels to catch onto stirrups. Now, they were about to be turned into soup. Reluctantly, he handed them over.

"They stink like my feet," he told her.

He hoped Virginia would take a sniff and wouldn't want to eat them.

She said, "Yum! Toe-jam soup."

The boot soup tasted awful. They swallowed it down fast and then sat staring into the damp, smoking fire. Something flashed at the edge of the fire pit—a rock. Zeke picked it up, turning the stone in his fingers; it shimmered yellow in the light.

"Mrs. Reed," he said. "Look at this. I think it's gold!"

Margaret Reed sighed. "What good is gold to us? I wish it was bread."

But some small part of Zeke needed the hope this gold might bring. He needed a dream to keep him going. He wrapped it in a small piece of cloth and put it in his pocket.

"If we ever get away, I'm coming back for more," he said.

"I'm never coming back!" Virginia said. "Not even for gold."

Zeke pictured the ranch that a pot of gold could buy. He could ride Star Boy through those green Californian fields.

The next day, the storm cleared and snow began to melt in steady drips. With relief, Zeke and the Reeds crawled out of the smelly cabin. He stretched his arms up to the pale sun. Sunshine!

One of the teamsters approached Zeke, holding out a shaking hand.

"Please, please, can you spare a small piece of rawhide?" he said. Then he collapsed into the snowbank and just lay there.

"Elliot!" Zeke crouched down.

Keseberg plodded through the snow. His matted, curly beard now fell to his chest. He licked his lips. "I'll eat him when he's dead."

"Monster," Virginia muttered.

"He's not dead." Zeke started to drag the teamster into the Reed cabin.

Mary Ann's mother blocked the way. "We can't feed him. We don't have enough for our children."

"He's starving." Zeke slipped a sliver of rawhide into the unconscious teamster's hand. Mrs. Reed noticed but said nothing. Together they wrapped the man in a blanket and dragged him back to his lean-to shelter.

Early the next morning, Zeke headed for the lean-to. But the teamster had disappeared. A trail through the snow led to Keseberg's shelter.

Zeke steeled himself and peered inside. The place smelled rank. Bloody. The teamster's body lay twisted in the corner. There was a long gash across his chest. Zeke reeled back. Had Keseberg killed Elliot?

Keseberg crouched at a fire pit, stirring a big, bubbling pot. He gave his carnivorous grin. "Want to join me?"

"He was one of us," Zeke said.

Keseberg shrugged. "You do what you got to do. Or else you die."

"There's got to be another way."

"You let me know when you find it. I'm not going to sit here, starving to death."

Zeke turned away. *I'll try fishing again. I saw those fish. It must be possible, surely, to catch them.*

As he plowed away through the snow, the flash came—one of the worst images he'd ever seen:

Keseberg sat at the fire, stirring his big black pot. Beside him, two human skulls, bashed open as if with rocks, grinned horribly. "Come and try it," Keseberg said. "Best thing I've ever tasted."

Zeke gulped a deep breath, trying to wipe the image from his mind.

That night, a scratching sound made him jolt awake in terror. Was Keseberg coming after them?

In the darkness, Mrs. Reed whispered, "Someone's trying to get in."

The sound came louder. Something was ripping at the rawhides.

A wild howl split the night.

"Wolves!" Zeke said. "It's wolves." He grabbed the rifle and fired two shots at the roof. "Get!" he shouted. "Get!"

There were shuffling sounds. Then silence.

Hungry, predatory wolves.

Hungry, predatory Keseberg.

How long could the pioneers hope to survive?

CHAPTER 14

December 1846
Truckee Lake (Now called Donner Lake)
Eastern Slopes of the Sierra Nevada

"Two more teamsters died yesterday," Zeke said. "How long do you think before help arrives?

Stanton looked glum. "Maybe not until late spring. No one at Sutter's Fort even knows we're stuck at Truckee Lake. When I left the Fort, Captain Sutter said I'd probably find you camped for winter at a lower elevation. And Reed thought you'd have Patrick Breen's whole herd for meat and milk."

Zeke stared at him in dismay. "I wish. Someone has to get through to the Fort. We have to tell Captain Sutter that people are dying here."

"No point trying, son. We've already sent four teams, but they haven't been able to cross the mountains."

Frustration filled him. What on earth could he do? The deep snow made walking impossible.

Just then Luis, one of the Miwok Indians, walked across the snow toward them. Zeke stared amazed at the two-foot-long contraptions under his feet.

"Wow! Look at that!"

Stanton nodded. "Snowshoes. The Indians use them. Luis built the frames using wood from the ox-bows and made lattice coverings out of oxhide strips."

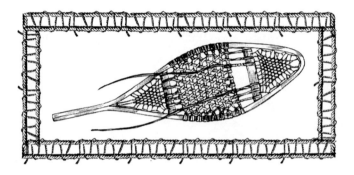

"They're great!" For the first time in what seemed like forever, Zeke felt a ray of hope. "With those, we can cross the mountain!"

"It's not easy to walk in those things," Stanton cautioned. "I'm not sure how far you'd get. They take a lot of energy. You'd have to be strong and healthy."

Zeke grinned. "Let's start making them!"

Seventeen people, mostly teens and young adults, volunteered to construct snowshoes and attempt the crossing. Weak with starvation but buoyed with hope, they persuaded Mr. Breen to donate one of his remaining rawhides and spent a week furiously making snowshoes.

Thrilled, Zeke found he could struggle across the snow and not sink right into it.

"Okay, Mule!" he told Lemuel. "You ready to walk to Sutter's Fort? We'll bring back food and a rescue party and we'll get everyone out of here."

"Let's do this," Lemuel said.

Mrs. Reed handed Zeke one of James Reed's hunting knives. "I want you to have this, son." With tears in her eyes, she then pressed a small, cloth-wrapped ball into his hand. "A treat. Save it for Christmas."

"Thank you. I'll open it after I've gathered a rescue party at Sutter's Fort." Zeke buried the gift deep in a pocket and grasped the knife's bone handle firmly.

On the sixteenth of December, ten men and five women, the strongest members of the Donner party, headed for the Sierra Nevada summit. Most were in their teens and twenties. Zeke, Lemuel, and Mary Ann were among the teenagers. Lemuel's brother, ten-year-old Billy, had no snowshoes but insisted on going too.

Mary Ann named the group *The Forlorn Hope*.

"You could have chosen a better name," Zeke commented. "Maybe something a little more optimistic?"

CHAPTER 15

December 1846
The Sierra Nevada Mountains

"Come on, Mule," Zeke joked, watching Lemuel and Mary Ann struggle to walk on snowshoes. "Don't be a slowpoke."

Lemuel prodded him with his hiking stick and laughed.

They were on their way. It felt good to be doing something useful at last.

Before leaving, the Donner Party members had pooled together enough rations to feed the Forlorn Hope for six days. Stanton said it would take less than that to reach Sutter's Fort. As long as the snow held off, they'd make it.

Balancing awkwardly on snowshoes, lifting and thumping down his feet, he pushed on, fell, and even crawled. Wet. Cold. Freezing. Deep snow covered the trail past yawning chasms, dizzy precipices, and deep canyons. Only one thing mattered—getting to Sutter's Fort.

A pale sun reflected on the snow and hurt his eyes. Stanton had warned about snow blindness. Zeke half closed his lids and pulled down the broad brim of his hat.

That first night, wrapped in blankets, he, Lemuel, Mary, and Billy boiled small strips of beef to make soup. Already weak from months of hunger, they passed around the little pot and took slow sips. Nearby, Zeke could see the other Forlorn Hope members shivering over fires, too.

Mary sighed. "We've trekked for ten hours. But we haven't gotten very far. Maybe three or four miles."

"My legs feel broken," Lemuel said.

"It's hard to walk on these heavy things," Zeke said. "But we'll get used to them."

Little Billy piped up looking scared and exhausted. "I'm going back."

"You can't," Lemuel told his brother. "You'll get lost."

All night, a ferocious gale roared. The next morning it still raged, buffeting Zeke, trying to push him back down the mountain. Ahead, the Sierra Nevada summit, a 7,200-foot-high mountain peak, loomed.

Fat snowflakes fell.

Silent.

Merciless.

"We still have to climb that peak," Mary Ann croaked through dry lips. Her long dark hair hung in icicles. "Look at us, we can barely walk."

"Put one foot in front of the other," Zeke said. "To stop is to die."

"We have to go on." Even on snowshoes, Lemuel tried to move with his usual swagger, but his eyes betrayed him. Zeke knew that, like himself, Lemuel was afraid.

They struggled upward.

"My little brother's gone," Lemuel said.

"Billy's gone? What do you mean?" Zeke said.

"Last night, he snuck off back the way we came with one of the teamsters. If he gets lost, Ma will kill me."

Mary Ann's voice cracked. "We're all lost anyway. Even the Indian guides are lost!"

Zeke looked around desperately. In the haze of falling snowflakes, all the snow-covered peaks looked the same. What if they never got out of this terrible maze? What if they couldn't find their way forward or back?

"Keep moving," he said. "If we don't, everyone back at the lake will starve." He thought of all those people he knew well, children and adults, starving at Truckee Lake, and he shuddered. At least sixty people had pinned their hopes on Zeke's party getting through the pass.

Could they cross the Sierra Nevada?

Maybe.

Maybe not.

How long could they keep going? The slippery mountains were smothered with snow. And still it drifted down.

As darkness fell, the temperature plummeted. The slope grew steeper, the sky blacker, and they were forced to stop.

Zeke trembled with hunger. They had nothing left to eat.

He rummaged in his pack, found the flint, and managed to set fire to the brittle top of a dead pine poking out of the snow. They all collapsed around the flames.

"Happy Christmas Eve," Zeke said. "Santa's reindeer would be a welcome sight."

Mary Ann shot him a smile that reminded him of better days. "Would you really eat Dasher and Dancer?" she said through blue lips.

"Yeah," Zeke said. "Roast venison. Yum!"

"We're all going to die unless we eat something real soon," grunted Foster, one of the family leaders. His bushy hair rose straight up from his head, making him look like a crazed scientist.

An Irish teamster doubled over. "Won't be long before one of us drops dead. When they do, the others should eat the body."

Zeke and Mary Ann exchanged nervous glances.

"Welcome to the Sierra Nevada Dining Room," Lemuel muttered. "Meat's on the menu again."

The burly Foster scanned the group. "Could be days before someone keels over. That'll be too late for us all. I say we draw sticks and eat the loser."

The group, as skinny as skeletons, stared at him with frightened eyes.

Horrified, Zeke shook his head. "No! We shouldn't do that."

"Keep quiet, you lunatic," Lemuel muttered. "Next thing, he'll eat you."

Cold, clammy fear crept down Zeke's spine. From the hungry look in Foster's wolf-like eyes, it was clear something terrible was going to happen. And it was going to happen soon.

He wished with all his heart he'd never joined the Donner Party.

CHAPTER 16

25th December 1846
Sierra Nevada Mountains Summit
Christmas Day

Zeke looked down at the endless tumbled, snow-covered mountains.

"We're as close as we'll ever get to Heaven." Mary Ann said.

"Or Hell," Zeke muttered.

He knew he should feel more hopeful since the Miwok Indians had found the mountain pass and guided them through, all of them struggling over the summit.

But as he stood on the western slopes of the Sierra Nevada, he felt worried. The snow had become drenching rain that pelted down. Hard. An icy torrential downpour that soaked everything.

Squinting, Zeke scanned the endless, desolate mountains ahead. They were in California, but this forsaken wilderness looked nothing like the grassy green Promised Land. The longed-for Sacramento River Valley was nowhere in sight.

"Does anyone have any idea where Sutter's Fort is?" Zeke looked hopefully at the Miwok Indians.

They shook their heads.

"What use are guides if they don't know the way," Foster growled.

Rain poured down. Did all the weather up here have to be so extreme?

"In all this rain, we'll never be able to light a fire," he said. "We're going to freeze our butts off."

That night, they pressed together under the blankets. The wind hurled rain and sleet.

In the grey dawn, wedged between the sweaty bodies of Lemuel and a Mexican teamster, Zeke heard a wild shout. He sprang up. Sleet stung his eyes and he struggled to keep upright. Snow was falling again. The infernal snow was everywhere.

Another shout rang out.

An Irish teamster stood in the falling snowflakes tearing off his clothes. "I'm hot!" he shouted. "I'm burning up."

"Calm down, brother." Zeke hauled him back under the blanket.

"I'm too hot," the teamster shouted. "Let go of me!" He pulled loose, ran out, and dove into a snowdrift.

"Get back here, you nutcase!" Zeke shouted. He felt weird, weak from hunger. His body warned him he was in danger: an about-to-expire-from-starvation sort of danger.

"There has to be something up here we can eat," he said.

Foster's eyes were cold and determined. "There is something."

Zeke thought of Keseberg's lair, the human bones in the bubbling pot. *Not this again.*

With hungry eyes, Foster watched the Irish teamster. The man now lay still and silent.

"We must eat what there is," Foster said, studying Zeke. "Or we'll all die."

"There must be game," Zeke said, his voice desperate.

"Only us," Foster replied.

Wincing, he turned to Mary Ann and whispered, "I think Foster's checking us out. I think if we stay we're dead meat."

"Don't forget he has the rifle," Mary Ann said.

"I'm not forgetting that," Zeke muttered. "I'm thinking of it every two minutes. We've got to get it from him."

"We could never do that. Never. Foster's a brute."

Mary Ann's father, the oldest member of the Forlorn Hope, whispered, "Listen to me, Mary Ann. If I die, I want you and your sister to take what you can."

With a sob, Mary Ann wrapped her arms around him. "No, Papa, no. Don't talk like that."

Her father's voice was weak and shaky. "I mean it, Mary Ann. Take what I can give you, my daughter. You must do anything you can to live. Anything. Promise me. You've got to get help for your mother. And the eight little ones too."

Zeke squeezed Mary Ann's hand. He knew her heart must be breaking. Her father was dying of starvation; would he even last the day? Zeke guessed what Mr. Graves was urging her to do, and he shuddered.

Beside him, Lemuel rocked to and fro. "Apple pie," he muttered. "Toast and jam, pancakes, chocolate pudding, roast beef and gravy and mashed potatoes." He slumped down in his blanket.

They'd have to start walking soon. Day was breaking.

Zeke closed his eyes. In his dream, he was eating a big juicy steak. The sound of crackling flames woke him. He smelled roasting meat. Yes! Had someone managed to snag a deer?

Meat!

Hunger roared like a beast in his stomach. His mouth filled with saliva.

Meat!

CHAPTER 17

December 1846
Western Slopes of the Sierra Nevada

Z eke crawled from his blanket and stood beneath the wind-whipped clouds that raced across the bleak sky. With a shock, he realized the day had come and gone. Evening was quickly falling.

A fire was burning in the forest some yards away. Foster and a small group were gathered around the blaze, which reached so high it sent twigs raining down from burning branches, covering the ground with flickering lights. It looked great. It smelled great.

"Come and eat!" Foster called. "Zeke! Mary Ann! All of you! Come and eat what we've been given."

Zeke staggered through the slush. Mary Ann stumbled after him.

Seven people, black silhouettes against the red glow,

crouched around a hissing fire, their backs to the flames and to one another. Something roasted in the embers.

"You've got meat!" Zeke cried.

No one replied. The seven at the fire chewed steadily, silently.

Mary Ann looked around wildly. "My father! Where is he?"

"Come," Mary Ann's sister took her arm. "Papa told us to do it. Papa wanted us to live. Come, Mary Ann."

Zeke shrank back. Were they really doing this?

Yes, they were.

"Eat," Foster commanded. "No one need eat their own kin. We lost three men tonight."

Zeke shook his head. So three had starved to death. He'd feared it but hadn't believed it would happen.

Foster approached. "Eat." His eyes were strange—distant. He held out a sharpened stick with a strip of burnt meat and offered it to Zeke. "Eat, or you could be the next to go."

Zeke, faint with hunger, found himself reaching out. He tried not to think about what he was about to do. He didn't want to starve to death. But he didn't want to do this either.

Was it wrong? It felt wrong. Very wrong. But if he died, his body would just rot in the snow. Wouldn't it be better if someone ate his body and lived? Did it matter? Mr. Graves had begged Mary Ann to do what she must. It was clear what her father had meant.

Zeke wanted to live. He had to do it. Gingerly, he took the sliver of burnt flesh and lifted it to his mouth. Then he gagged and dropped it. Turning, he vomited into the wet snow.

Not looking at him, Mary Ann lifted the sliver and began to chew.

"Zeke. You have to eat," Foster said. "Go fetch the others. We all have to eat."

Zeke looked back. Where was Lemuel? Nearby, the Miwok Indians crouched at their own fire. What were they making of all this?

Like silent shadows, the Indian guides rose. Blankets pulled tight around their shoulders, they slipped away into the dark. The Miwok were leaving!

Zeke made up his mind fast. The Miwok were his only chance at finding a trail. He'd leave now, too. Fumbling, he checked his belt. Reed's hunting knife was still there. Together with the small cloth bag Mrs. Reed had pressed into his hand when he'd left. *A treat,* she'd said. *Save it for Christmas.*

Well, it was Christmas. The worst Christmas he'd ever had. But she'd given him a treat. He'd kept his promise, sure it would be a small family keepsake. Only now did her words sink in. A treat . . .

Hands clumsy with anticipation, he untied the knot. Two slices of dried apple, a piece of bacon, and an inch of dried venison. Gratitude washed over him with the force of a tidal wave. Weak kneed, he lifted the venison to his nose and inhaled deeply. Softly, he whispered his thanks, thinking of Mrs. Reed and Virginia, all of them back at Truckee Lake.

"Lemuel!" he whispered, shaking Lemuel's shoulder. "I've got a treat for you here. Wake up!"

Lemuel groaned but didn't move.

"Come on, Mule," Zeke begged. "Come on! Please!"

"Zeke!" Foster's voice rang out. "Zeke!"

Zeke whirled around. Fear filled the mountains with dark shapes coming after him. Did Foster want more meat? Was Foster coming a-hunting? Hunting for him? *Was Foster the dangerous man he saw in the scary flash?*

Already, the Miwok Indians were out of sight. If he was

going to follow in their tracks, he'd have to hurry. He shook Lemuel harder but couldn't wake his friend.

Zeke slipped a piece of bacon into Lemuel's mouth and another into his own. "I'll be back with help, Mule," he said. "Hang in there."

The only signs of the Miwok were their snowshoe tracks across the dirty, melting snow. But when he reached a section of rocky shale, the tracks disappeared.

He raced along a mountain ridge and descended a deep canyon, walking sideways. Down, down he slid. The snowshoes made good sleds.

As he stood up, a pocket of snow gave way under his feet, and he sank almost to his armpits. Throwing out his arms, he managed to break the fall. Frantically, he tried to feel something solid, but below his feet was icy cold water. He'd fallen into a snow-covered stream.

With all his strength, he managed to heave himself up onto the snow. Numb with cold, he climbed another mountain as steep as the one he'd just descended. He drove the toes of his snowshoes into the loose snow. *One foot in front of the other. Just keep going.*

The snow became patchy, giving way to stiff grass and muddy slush. He took off his snowshoes and winced at the sight of his swollen bleeding feet.

He was glad to reach a pine thicket. Now he had some protection from the wind. Slowly chewing the dried venison, he looked for a place to spend the night.

Behind him, a branch snapped.

He whirled around.

And looked right into the eyes of a giant black bear.

CHAPTER 18

January 1847
Bear Valley, California

Zeke froze. Adrenalin flooded his veins.

He forced himself not to run. Somewhere in his blank, petrified mind, he remembered one thing: Never run from a wild animal. Everything in the wild runs faster than you.

The bear moved forward with heavy, methodical steps. It slammed its massive paw down on a branch, cracking the branch in half.

A warning?

A show of strength?

Zeke stared wide-eyed. He remembered something too late: Never look a bear or an attacking dog in the eye.

Oh, no.

The bear reared up on its hind legs. It was big. Monstrous.

Slowly, Zeke backed away.

The bear roared. Maybe it was a mother bear with cubs. Or maybe it was as hungry as he was. If that was the case, he was history.

Hoping to play dead, Zeke dropped face-first into the mud. He covered the back of his neck with his hands. *Okay, bear, I'm dead. Now just go away. Please.*

With a ferocious growl, the bear slammed down onto Zeke's back.

A sour smell wafted over him as its hot breath whooshed over his neck. The bear was crushing him and sort of nuzzling him. Was it sniffing him? Was it deciding if he smelled good enough to eat? He smelled sweaty. And human. Oh brother. Sweaty and human were probably a bear's favorite smells.

His heart thumped so hard he could hear it in his ears.

Snarling, the bear tore into his blanket. Teeth grazed his shoulder.

Then the bear rose.

Zeke's shoulder burned. Was the bear leaving?

No such luck.

Now he was being rag-dolled, suspended by the bear's teeth.

For a few seconds, he dangled there in horrified agony. Desperate, he tried to grab his hunting knife, but he couldn't reach it.

The bear dropped him.

Saliva dripped from pointed fangs, falling onto Zeke's prone body. The bear roared, jaws gaping. It was going to rip out his throat! Blood thundered in his ears. He flexed his fingers and heaved his body up. He had one desperate plan: gouge out the bear's eyes.

He managed to thrust one finger in, but it was an uneven match and made the bear more furious. With a bellowing growl, it sank its teeth into his leg. There was a horrible sound of teeth on bone.

Zeke screamed. A long, loud, agonized scream.

To his shock, the bear let go. It squealed like a stuck pig, lumbered sideways, and ran.

Moaning, he managed to pull himself up. The bear was galumphing down the trail. Stunned, he spotted the arrow jutting from its shoulder.

Another arrow whizzed by, hitting the bear's back.

Shouts came from the pine thicket. Five Indian braves ran out. Whooping, they chased the bear, loosing arrow after arrow.

The bear fell to the ground.

The Indians wasted no time. Still whooping, they leapt on the downed bear.

Zeke tried to get up and fell back groaning. Blood soaked through his breeches and jacket. He needed help, fast, but the Indians weren't even looking at him. They were busy skinning the bear, talking loudly, and obviously pleased with their kill.

Black flecks swarmed before Zeke's eyes. His head fell back, and everything went gray.

When he came around, two Indians were hauling him along, his feet dragging.

He blinked as an Indian village with cone-shaped hide and bark dwellings swam into view. Women and children in pale, deer-hide garments cheered and whooped at the sight of bear meat. A bundled-up toddler pointed at Zeke and began to shriek. Zeke passed out.

He came to again to find himself inside a cone-shaped

dwelling. A Native Indian woman with long black hair and a creased, leathery face bathed his wounded leg and shoulder.

"Is it bad?" he stammered, wincing with pain.

She motioned him to lie back. Then she covered the wounds with an herbal-smelling paste.

Zeke groaned. His shoulder throbbed. His leg throbbed. Then his stomach rumbled. Loud.

The Indian women made a noise that sounded like a *tut-tut*. She left the teepee and returned with a bowl filled with warm, starchy porridge.

"Thank you! Thank you!" Zeke dipped his fingers in and ate eagerly. It tasted great, like hickory smoke and corn.

A brave wearing red-feathered band around his forehead ducked in through the opening. He handed Zeke a slice of warm bear liver.

The liver had a strong meaty flavor. Chewing slowly, Zeke felt strength rushing back into his body. He bowed his head in thanks. The fur hide beneath him felt soft and he sighed. For the first time in months, he was well fed, warm, and comfortable. He drifted off into a deep, dreamless sleep.

Zeke woke to noises outside the teepee. He could hear the murmur of voices and the laughter of children. A drummer beat out a monotonous tattoo.

A roaring fire flickered somewhere nearby, sending shadows and light dancing in the tent and warming the chilly air. The warmth was delicious. He snuggled deeper into the fur hides.

Then he thought of the others. Of the Forlorn Hope—his

starving, freezing friends in the mountains. Of the scary-dangerous Keseberg and the starving pioneers at the lake.

Nervous energy swept through him.

He had to get help for them all.

He had to get to Sutter's Fort.

CHAPTER 19

19th February 1847
Truckee Lake (now called Donner Lake)
Nevada

For three long, desperate weeks, Zeke struggled to walk again, but his wounds were too deep.

Finally, with the Indians' help and a splint around his injured limb, his strength grew.

It had taken ages, though, and he still had a long way to go. He was terrified of what he'd find by the time he brought help.

So it seemed like a miracle when men from Sutter's Fort arrived at the Indian Village looking for a guide to Truckee Lake. Seven men on mules; the First Relief had finally come looking for the lost Donner Party.

Zeke staggered out to meet them, quickly relating the whole, awful story.

"Onward, then," a man said. "Who here will guide us?"

But the Indians flatly refused.

Looking up at the snow-covered Sierra Nevada, Zeke understood why. These were Miwok Indians, just like the two Donner Party guides who still hadn't returned—Luis and Salvadore.

Zeke's leg still hurt, but he had to grab this chance. "I'll take you," he said. "I know the way."

The men eyed his wounded leg, talked to one another, and then accepted his offer. They hiked for days. The trek up the mountains was near impossible. The mules couldn't make it through the still-deep snow, and three men turned back, refusing to continue on foot.

Finally, waist-deep in snow, Zeke stood again on the Sierra Nevada's eastern slopes.

He leaned on his hiking sticks and rested his wounded leg, gazing down at Truckee Lake. It looked like a ghost camp. He saw no people, no movement. No sign his friends still lived.

"There're sixty people down there?" Glover, a grizzled-faced man, said.

"Yep. It's all downhill from here." Got to sound cheerful, he thought, keep the troops upbeat. They had no idea what awaited them. "Let's go!"

"Looks to me like they're all dead."

One man, pale with exhaustion, said, "I'm about dead myself. We're wasting our time climbing down there."

"No, sir! We have to go down," Zeke said. "There are men, women, and lots of small children, all starving."

Sliding sideways, the five made their way down to the camp. The first thing Zeke noticed was the rank smell.

"Anyone here?" Glover shouted.

"Mrs. Reed!" Zeke shouted. "Virginia!"

He stumbled over something. A snow-covered branch? No. Human bones, partly buried in snow. He reeled back. Who had died? And why were their bones scattered like this? Where was Keseberg? He shuddered.

"Oh gosh," Glover groaned. "A terrible thing has gone on here."

A woman staggered out of the Reed cabin. Zeke hardly recognized Mrs. Reed, Once attractive and smartly-dressed, she looked like a bag of bones wrapped in rags.

She stared, rubbing her sunken eyes. Her voice trembled. "Are you men from California, or do you come from heaven?"

"Captain Sutter sent us," Glover said. His voice was soft, reassuring. "We're the First Relief party. We've come to help."

She staggered and then her voice rose in a high, excited scream. "Help has come! Help has come!"

Relief washed over Zeke when Virginia, Patty, Jimmy, and Tommy crawled out of the cabin. He hardly recognized the three. Their eyes were much too large for their pinched faces, while their arms and legs were like sticks.

Virginia grabbed hold of Zeke's jacket. "Zeke! You came back to us! Did you bring food?"

Jimmy stood blinking rapidly. "Is it really you, Zeke?"

Zeke dipped into a sack and took out handfuls of hard biscuits. The children grabbed them, cramming them into their mouths.

"Careful. Eat slowly," he said.

Zeke hugged Jimmy, wincing at how sharp his bones felt. His heart leapt when he saw Lemuel's little brother, Billy, stumbling toward him. When Billy fled the Forlorn Hope, he'd thought he'd never see him again.

"Billy! You made it back."

"Yes. I sure did." Billy's eyes were focused on the relief party. "Where's Lemuel? Is he with you?"

Zeke shook his head. "No. I never made it to Sutter's Fort, but I hope he did."

Starving men, women, and children grabbed the dried jerky and biscuits. All looked ghastly, their skin drawn tight over bones. Many looked like wild animals, their expressions fierce.

He and the rescuers couldn't possibly help more than forty weak people climb the Sierra Nevada. With an awful feeling of dread and guilt, he realized they could only take the strongest.

"Eat slowly," Glover warned them. "Or you'll be sick. We couldn't carry all the food, but we've cached some on the trail."

"Where's my papa?" Virginia said.

Mrs. Reed clutched Zeke's arm. "Is my husband alive? Did he send you?"

"Captain Sutter sent us, ma'am," Glover said. "Some people from that group you sent out arrived at the fort and told Captain Sutter there were starving people at Truckee Lake. We haven't seen your husband."

Lemuel's mother hobbled up. "Where's my son? Is he safe? Did all the Forlorn Hope make it to Sutter's Fort with you?"

Zeke shook his head. "I didn't get to Sutter's Fort, Mrs. Murphy. I don't know who got there. I got as far as Bear Valley. Then I was attacked by a bear. I ended up in an Indian village. The First Relief passed through last week looking for a guide. So here I am."

"You got attacked by a bear!" Little Jimmy looked much livelier now that he'd eaten something. "Was it a big one?"

"Yeah, a big one." Zeke grinned at him. He'd bring Jimmy

safely through the Sierra Nevada even if he had to carry him. "You ready to be the youngest kid ever to walk across the Sierra Nevada summit?"

"Yeah! But Tommy will be the youngest. We have to bring Tommy too."

Zeke turned to four-year-old Tommy, who looked weak and sickly, and the weight of their situation crushed down on him. There were so many young children at Truckee Lake. They'd have to be carried, and there simply weren't enough adults to carry them all to safety.

"Thank God you brought these men here." Mrs. Reed clutched his hand. "Bless you, Zeke. Your papa will be proud of you." Tears brimmed in her eyes. "Seventeen more poor souls have died here since you left. I don't know how many are still alive. I was sure my family was going to die. You have to help me get my children through the mountains, Zeke. I'll never be able to do it alone."

"I will," Zeke promised.

But what of Lemuel's family and the rest? With a feeling of impending doom, he stared at the brooding sky. He'd seen too many of those swollen clouds. He knew what was coming: another ghastly snowstorm. This place could surprise in the worst ways.

He thought about Mrs. Reed's words. Would Pa be proud of him? At the moment, he didn't care. If he could get some of these people over the mountains to Sutter's Fort, he'd be proud of himself.

Little Patty was handing out biscuits, a big smile on her face. She still had her treasured doll tucked inside her apron pocket. Mrs. Reed had shared their food with him, and James Reed had trusted him to help his family. Zeke would do everything to honor that trust.

"We have to hurry, Mrs. Reed. Another storm's rolling in. We have to leave. Now!"

"Now?" Mrs. Reed looked confused.

Glover nodded. "Faster the better, ma'am. If snow closes the pass, we'll all be stuck again. Gather what you and the children need." He turned to the four volunteers. "Search the cabins. Find the strongest—those who can walk out on their own. Hurry."

Zeke stomped from cabin to cabin. He winced, seeing how frail and strange the starving pioneers had become. Some appeared totally mad, talking to themselves and grasping at unseen objects in the air.

At the Graves' cabin, Mary Ann's two teenage sisters hobbled to him. "Zeke! You came to save us."

Their mother followed, her younger children clinging to her skirts. She tried to peer around him. "Where's Mary Ann? And my husband? Are they with you?"

Zeke thought of Mr. Graves dying of starvation in the snow. He pressed his lips shut. What good would it do to tell her now?

"I don't know who got to the fort, ma'am," he said.

"Please take my older girls with you." She looked with hope-less eyes at her small children. "I'll stay here with my little ones." As she spoke, she wrapped a blanket around each teenager's shoulders and kissed their cheeks again and again. "Stay strong," she whispered. "I'll see you again. Stay strong."

He approached Keseberg's lean-to reluctantly. It was a scene from hell, the scene from his terrible flash. Two human skulls, cracked open as though bashed with rocks, stared from empty eye sockets. Scattered bones lay piled in the far corner. Where had Keseberg gotten them? Was he a killer?

He found Keseberg seated at his fire pit. "I injured my foot," he growled. "I can't walk. I'll stay here till the snow clears."

Zeke left without a word.

He ran to the nearest Donner tent and found George Donner lying injured and unconscious. The five Donner girls turned, and their faces lit up. "Zeke, you brought help."

Zeke handed Mrs. Donner a small sack of biscuits. Her face was wan but determined.

"I can't leave my husband," she said. "Please, take my oldest daughters. They're strong girls, they'll be able to walk out."

"I'll take care of them," he promised. "But ma'am, stay away from Mr. Keseberg. He's dangerous."

Face filled with grief, she nodded and hugged her eldest daughters.

As they left, the two younger girls ran after him. One, around five, grabbed his hand. "Please take us, Zeke. Please."

"I'm sorry, but I can't," Zeke said. He felt awful. "The snow is too deep. It would be right up to your chests. And there aren't enough men to carry you."

The three-year-old girl sucked her thumb and began to cry.

The five-year-old wrapped her arms around her baby sister and whispered, "Don't cry, Eliza, we can follow them. I'll find the way."

Zeke's heart ached. He knelt before them. "More men are coming soon, Eliza. They'll be able to carry you both."

He prayed it was true.

Soon the small group of survivors stumbled out of the camp. None of them looked able to make the trek.

Zeke glanced back. Families had gathered to watch them go. He could hardly bear to wave goodbye to the desperate, miserable people left behind.

"Stay safe," he whispered.

CHAPTER 20

22nd February 1847
The Sierra Nevada

Hurricane-force winds began to blow as the First Relief members led the pioneers up the pass. On the high ridges, pines crashed down, making Zeke cringe. Again, the storm gods were set to destroy them.

Four-year-old Tommy let go of his mother's hand and collapsed in the snow. "I can't walk, Mama. My toes hurt."

"We can't stop." Zeke, already carrying a toddler, lifted Tommy on to his back. Pain shot through his wounded leg.

"My toes are frozen," Patty said. "My toes hurt really bad."

Glover shook his head. "This isn't going to work, Mrs. Reed. I'll have to take these two young ones back, ma'am."

Patty looked up at her mother.

Mrs. Reed looked anguished. "We'll all go back."

"No, ma'am," Glover said. "I'll take these two youngsters

back. Mrs. Murphy will care for them. It won't take long, and I promise I'll return with the second relief party to collect them."

Patty hugged her mother. "If you never see me again, Mama, do the best you can."

Mrs. Reed held Patty and Tommy both for a long time. Then the burly figure of Glover, pulling along the two children, disappeared into the haze. Tears slid down Mrs. Reed's face.

Zeke swallowed hard.

As darkness fell, they reached the tree where they'd cached a sack of food. But to Zeke's horror, the sack was ripped apart and empty.

After a miserable night they trekked on, moving as fast as possible and fearing the next storm. Those without snowshoes followed in the tracks of the men who had them. Zeke winced when he saw Billy's bleeding feet. They were so swollen with frostbite that he couldn't fit into his shoes, forcing the ten-year-old to walk barefoot over snow and rocks.

"Hey, Billy. Keep it up," he urged. "Lemuel will be happy to see you."

Meanwhile, five-year-old Jimmy Reed's legs were too short to follow in the men's footprints. He placed his knees on the mounded snow and climbed over.

"You can do it, Jimmy," Zeke told him, pulling him along. "Every step you're getting closer."

Jimmy grinned. His teeth looked too big in his gaunt face. "I'm getting closer to Pa. But I'm real hungry."

"I know. I'm hungry too." Zeke gave Jimmy and the toddler he was carrying two of his snowshoe laces to chew.

Glover cut strips from his fringed buckskin jacket and handed them around.

At the summit pass, Zeke took a deep, relieved breath. Thank goodness it was still open. Everyone watched the overhanging snowdrifts with fearful eyes as they staggered through the narrow canyon.

"Only seventy miles to go!" Zeke said.

"Seventy more miles," Virginia croaked. "With nothing to eat."

But then they neared Bear Valley, and a welcome shout rang out. "Food!"

Glover pointed at a fallen pine. This time the cached food was still safely buried in the snow. The hard biscuits tasted delicious, the beef jerky even better.

Ten-year-old William Hook grabbed a handful. "I want more!"

"No more now," Zeke warned. "You'll get sick." Carefully, he hung the sack from a high branch.

But the next morning, Zeke awoke to see William Hook on the ground, rolling in pain.

"He ate all the beef jerky," Jimmy whispered. "I saw him climb the tree and sneak it in the middle of the night."

"He ate the beef jerky?" Zeke ran to look. *What the heck!* The beef jerky was gone. We needed that food!

Then William stopped rolling and just lay there.

Glover rushed over. He pressed down on the boy's chest and breathed air into his mouth. The rest of the party watched, stunned.

Eventually, Glover got to his feet and shook his head. "He's gone." Turning away, he muttered, "Poor starving kid managed to die of overeating."

No one spoke.

A man searched William's pockets and took what remained of the biscuits and beef jerky. Then, silently, they buried him.

CHAPTER 21

23nd February 1847
The Sierra Nevada

T he next day, when they reached the western slopes, Zeke heard shouting. A bearded mountain-man was riding a mule up toward them. Behind him came fourteen men with horses, mules, and sacks of provisions.

Zeke, exhausted and hungry, staggered in relief.

"Papa! Papa!" Virginia shouted. "I knew you'd come to save us."

With shouts of joy, Mrs. Reed, Virginia, and Jimmy limped to meet James Reed, throwing their arms around him.

His face shining with joy, Reed hugged them. Then he looked around. "Where's Patty? And my little Tommy?"

Mrs. Reed began to sob. "They had to go back to Truckee Lake, James. They couldn't make it up the mountain."

"Patty and Tommy are alone at Truckee Lake?" Reed looked grim.

Zeke knew how he must feel, for thoughts of Patty and Tommy, along with little Eliza Donner and her baby sister, haunted him.

These men would bring them out. They'd bring all of them out.

"I'll take you to Sutter's Fort," Reed continued. "Once it's in sight and I know you're safe, I'll go back for Patty and Tommy."

The flash came fast: *He stood in the Reed cabin at Truckee Lake, looking down at poor Mrs. Murphy. She lay still, surrounded by starving children. A dark shadow entered, looming over them all. Keseberg. The monster with his filthy beard took Tommy's hand.*

"I'll take care of this boy, Mrs. Murphy," Keseberg said. "You've got too many young ones to take care of."

"No," Zeke gasped. "No!"

Reed stared at him. "What's the matter, Cecil? What is it?"

Keseberg's hungry smile was locked in his mind.

"You have to go to Truckee Lake right now, sir," Zeke stammered. "Immediately."

Reed looked impatient. "I'm taking Mrs. Reed to safety first."

Fear numbed Zeke's brain. He pictured Keseberg's cabin, pictured the human bones in the big black pot. He knew, just knew, what happened there.

Zeke grabbed the man's arm. "No. Please, you've got to get there as fast as you can. Tommy's in danger, sir. Terrible danger. I know. I saw it."

"What are you talking about, boy? You saw it?" Reed shook his head. "I have no time for this nonsense, Cecil. You sound crazy."

"I tell you, I saw it," Zeke repeated. "Tommy is in danger from Keseberg."

"How can you possibly know that?" Reed asked.

"Papa!" Virginia cried. "You have to listen to Zeke, Papa. He can see things. I know he can."

Stunned, Zeke stared at her.

"You're both sounding crazy," Reed said.

But now Jimmy joined in. "Pa! Zeke knows. I heard him tell Patty and Edward not to race. He knew someone would get hurt. And they were. And I heard him tell Snyder to be careful, but he wasn't and now Snyder's dead. Please listen, Pa."

Zeke found his voice. "Keseberg is taking Tommy to his lean-to. I know it. And Keseberg is a cannibal. Tommy is in terrible danger, sir!"

Mrs. Reed's face turned a ghastly shade of pale. "Please listen to him, James," she begged. "Please get Tommy and Patty away from there. We'll be fine, Zeke will get us to safety."

Reed took a step back and studied his family. "All right," he said slowly. "I'll go immediately."

Zeke heaved a sigh of relief. For once, the flashes would do some good. And Mrs. Reed, Virginia, and Jimmy didn't think he was weird.

He watched the family say goodbye, and for a moment, he felt alone. But he thought of his own family. They'd always had food on the table and clothes on their backs. Maybe his pa cared in his own way. Maybe this tough journey had changed both of them enough to sort out their differences. One thing he knew, he had a loving mother; he was lucky for that. Even his brother could be fun sometimes. And after the struggles he'd waged, he bet he could beat his brother with one arm tied behind his back.

The Second Relief men approached, handing out bread. Eagerly, he joined their circle and took a chunk.

"It smells wonderful." It tasted even better, soft in the middle, crusty on the outside. "Wow, I really missed bread."

The sound of a familiar horse's neigh startled him. He swallowed so fast he nearly choked.

Nearby stood a horse with a star on his forehead. *Star Boy?* No, how could it be? He looked closer and his head spun.

"Star Boy!" he shouted. "Star Boy!"

The horse snorted. With ears pricked up, he cantered up to Zeke and nuzzled at his hand.

"Star Boy!" Zeke stammered. "Where did you come from?" He turned to Reed, who was making his last preparations to leave. "Sir! I think this horse is mine! Where did you find him?"

"In the Forty Mile Desert. I bought him from some Paiute Indians," Reed said. "So it's true? I thought he could be. Same star." He stroked Star Boy's mane. "My mare had injured her hoof. Star Boy carried me over the Sierra Nevada all the way to Sutter's Fort. He's a great horse."

Mr. Reed settled little Jimmy into Star Boy's saddle. "How

about you take Star Boy to the fort with you, Cecil? He's your horse again. It's my thanks to you for taking care of my family."

"I will, sir. Thank you, sir!" Zeke gave him a wide smile. "I'm sure glad to see my horse, sir!"

Joy filled him. Star Boy was back at his side.

CHAPTER 22

SUTTER'S FORT

March 1847
Sacramento Valley
California

I t was spring in California. Zeke had never seen anything more beautiful. Warm blue sky and sunshine made the Sacramento River sparkle. The valley, golden with rippling fields of poppies, stretched out before him. Heat loosened his muscles and he breathed in deeply.

Soon, the adobe walls of Sutter's Fort came into view. Those high walls, guarded by soldiers and cannons, shielded cozy homes, fertile orchards, and even ranches with fat cattle, horses, and sheep.

It felt like a dream. Food. Safety. Warmth.

His family would be inside, and surely his friends would have arrived by now. He longed to see Lemuel, Mary Ann, and Edward.

"Almost there," he said to Virginia and Jimmy.

"I can't relax until I know Patty and Tommy are safe." Virginia shuddered. "Oh, Zeke, I pray Papa got there in time to save them."

"I know Papa will save them," Jimmy said.

"Yes. I think he will," Zeke said.

He could picture Reed riding as fast as he could, stomping through the snow, charging into the Reed cabin. And he pictured Patty and Tommy running into his arms. Patty would have fought to protect Tommy; she would have done whatever she could to save her little brother from the cannibal's lair.

For once in Zeke's life, his warning had been heeded, and he felt sure Reed would get there in time.

"It's been a terrible journey." Virginia drew a deep breath. "Why did it go so wrong, Zeke? It was fun when we started."

"It was, we saw some pretty amazing things," he said.

"But there should be a warning on the Oregon Trail to any settlers heading west."

"Saying what?"

Virginia met his eyes. "Never take no cut-offs and hurry along as fast as you can."

Zeke shot her a wry smile.

"We've become hardy pioneers, haven't we?" Virginia said.

He glanced up to where Jimmy sat astride Star Boy, eyes fastened on the fort ahead. Zeke patted the small boy's skinny leg. "We sure have. Anything will seem easy after what we've been through!"

At long last, a grin lightened Virginia's face.

Zeke thought about the gold nugget he'd found in the firepit. "I'm going back there. When the weather changes, I'm going to search for gold. Then I'm going to buy a ranch and breed horses with stars on their foreheads."

She nodded. "If anyone can, you will. I wish you the best, Zeke Farnsworth."

He stroked Star Boy's silky mane and whispered, "We did it, Star Boy! You and me. We survived the westward trek, we survived the Donner Party. We escaped!"

WHAT HAPPENED TO THE DONNER PARTY SURVIVORS?

Here, Dear Reader, is what happened to the pioneers whose lives we've been following in this book:

James Reed arrived at Truckee Lake in time to save his children, Patty and Tommy. The Reed family survived, and they adopted two orphaned Donner girls. Reed struck it rich during the Californian Gold Rush, and his family settled on a 500-acre ranch in San Jose. The Reed School in San Jose is named after Reed's grandson, Fraser Reed.

Virginia Reed married the young pioneer who built the original Truckee Lake log cabin. They had nine children. Virginia became a noted businesswoman in fire insurance in California. As a well-known equestrian, she won many prizes for horsemanship. Virginia Street in San Jose is named after her.

Patty (Martha) Reed and her husband had eight children. The doll she took with her on the Donner Party expedition can be seen at the Sutter's Fort Museum in Sacramento. Martha Street in San Jose is named after her.

Jimmy and Tommy Reed prospected for gold during the Gold Rush, and bred horses with their father in San Jose, California.

The **Breen family** parents and seven children lived in San Juan Bautista, California. Their home, the Castro-Breen Adobe, is a historical landmark. Patrick Breen wrote a diary detailing the Donner Party travels. Edward Breen became a prominent rancher and noted horseman.

Eliza Donner wrote a fascinating book called *The Expedition Of The Donner Party And Its Tragic Fate*. Eliza's husband became the mayor of San Jose and a noted politician.

Billy Murphy grew up an orphan at Sutter's Fort. Billy studied law and became a lawyer and District Attorney of Yuba County.

Mary Ann Graves married five months after reaching California. Her first husband was murdered. She remarried and had seven children.

Lewis Keseberg was accused of murdering Tamsen Donner and others. He admitted to eating the bodies but denied killing anyone. The charge of murder could not be proven, but people shunned him.

William Foster prospected for gold during the gold rush. He owned a store on the Yuba River, where Foster's Bar is named after him.

And, according to our story, **Zeke Farnsworth** was reunited with his friends at Sutter's Fort. He prospected for gold and bought a two-hundred-acre ranch near Monterey, California. He became a noted horseman, and he bred horses with white stars on their foreheads.

DONNER PARTY SURVIVOR QUOTES

Never take no cut-offs and hurry along as fast as you can.
    — *Virginia Reed in a letter to her cousin*

Mr. Bridger informs me that the route we design to take is a fine level road with plenty of water and grass
    — *James F. Reed, letter from Fort Bridger, July 31, 1846*

Despair drove many nearly frantic. The farther we went up, the deeper the snow got. The wagons could not go. The mules kept falling down in the snow head foremost, and the Indian said he could not find the road.
    — *Virginia Reed*

They thought that as I was so small and light, I could walk in their snow shoe tracks. It soon became manifest that I could not, so I went back.
    — *William "Billy" Murphy*

I was awakened by a scratching sound over my head . . . it was the wolves trying to get into the cabin to eat me and the dead
    — *Lewis Keseberg*

William "Billy" Murphy, 10

The relief had left part of their provisions on top of the mountain, thinking to have it on their return—but lo and behold there was nothing there — *William Graves*

O Mary I have not wrote you half of the trouble we have had but I have wrote you enough to let you know that you don't know what trouble is but thank god we have all got through and the only family that did not eat human flesh.

— *Patty Reed, 12, in a letter to her cousin*

Christmas was near . . . my mother had determined weeks before that her children should have a treat on this one day. She had laid away a few dried apples, some beans, a bit of tripe, and a small piece of bacon. When this hoarded store was brought out, the delight of the little ones knew no bounds . . . So bitter was the misery relieved by that one bright day, that I have never since sat down to a Christmas dinner without my thoughts going back to Donner Lake

— *Virginia Reed*

I will now give you some good and friendly advice. Stay at home.

— Mary Ann Graves in a letter to her relatives

10 FAST FACTS ABOUT THE DONNER PARTY

1. The wagon train set out on their westward trek dangerously late in the season
2. By taking an ill-advised cutoff, instead of saving time, they added nearly a month to their journey
3. The unfortunate settlers lost the race against the winter snowfall by only a few days
4. Food supplies and livestock were lost along the trail, leaving them with nothing to eat
5. Most survivors were children and teenagers
6. A small party called the 'Forlorn Hope' set out for help on makeshift snowshoes
7. There were four different rescue efforts by relief teams from Sutter Fort who attempted to bring out the starving pioneers, which took over two months
8. The last pioneer rescued, Lewis Keseberg, was accused of murder but the charges were never proven
9. Abraham Lincoln nearly joined the Donner Party. A friend of James Reed, he eventually decided against it as his wife was pregnant and didn't want to make the journey.
10. Only two families survived the ordeal intact: the Reeds and the Breens, who made it to California without a suffering single death

WESTWARD EXPANSION, THE GOLD RUSH, AND THE OREGON TRAIL

DONNER MEMORIAL STATE PARK

The State of California created the Donner Memorial State Park at Donner Lake (formerly Truckee Lake) in 1927. The Emigrant Trail tells the history of westward migration into California.

The Murphy cabin and Donner monument were established as a National Historic Landmark in 1963. A bronze plaque commemorates the Donner Party members, indicating who survived and who did not. The park receives around 200,000 visitors a year.

WESTWARD EXPANSION (1801 TO 1861)

In 1803, the United States purchased nearly a million square miles of territory from the French. The land stretched west from the Mississippi River to the Rocky Mountains. And from the Gulf of Mexico, it extended north to Canada. The purchase, known as the Louisiana Territory, doubled the size of the United States and strengthened the young country.

Pioneers saw this as an opportunity to acquire land to farm and mine. Settlers began to head west in earnest, traveling in large wagon trains that stretched for miles. Americans felt it was their duty to expand west, and this belief was called manifest destiny. However this led to Native Americans losing their land, causing war and strife between the settlers and the peoples of the west.

Through their labors and accomplishments, pioneers helped define the character of America. Seeking opportunities and happiness, families faced hardships and danger to build new communities.

THE GOLD RUSH

This westward expansion was accelerated by the Gold Rush and mining opportunities when gold was found at Sutter's Mill in1848. The discovery of gold brought approximately 300,000 people to California from the rest of the United States and abroad.

THE OREGON TRAIL AND THE CALIFORNIA TRAIL

The Oregon Trail is a 2,170-mile (3,490 km) east-west wagon route from Missouri through Kansas, Nebras-ka, Wyoming, Colorado, Utah, Idaho, all the way to Oregon. It was built by fur trappers and traders, but soon became the primary western migration route, used by over 400,000 settlers. Into wild country went hunters, trappers, fur traders, gold miners, soldiers, surveyors, and farmers. The covered wagons that carried the pioneers became known as prairie schooners or ships of the plains as the wind blew their canvas tops.

Annual improvements were made, including bridges and easier cutoffs. One of the trail's offshoots was the California Trail, which split away from the Oregon Trail in Fort Hall, Idaho, and ended at Sutter's Fort, California.

Download the study guide at:
https://www.subscribepage.com/escaped-donner

AUTHORS' NOTE

The Donner Party expedition is one of the most gripping tragedies in U.S. pioneer history. The name Donner Party evokes creepy images of cannibalism, of starving pioneers eating one another in the terrible Sierra Nevada winter. But writing the book, we realized that these pioneers were simply people like ourselves.

The hopeful settlers were following their dream of a new life in the west. The Donner Party members were adventurous, brave, and enthusiastic. They made ill-advised choices, and they were terribly unlucky. The unfortunate group was trapped in an impossibly dangerous situation.

Of the eighty-seven pioneers who set out, half were under eighteen years of age. Of the forty-five survivors, thirty-two were children and teenagers. That incredible fact shows the courage and determination of the young pioneers. This book is our tribute to them.

THE I ESCAPED BOOKS

I Escaped North Korea!

I Escaped The California Camp Fire

I Escaped The World's Deadliest Shark Attack

I Escaped Amazon River Pirates

I Escaped The Donner Party

Coming soon

I Escaped The Salem Witch Trials

MORE BOOKS BY ELLIE CROWE

Kamehameha: The Boy Who Became a Warrior King

Nelson Mandela—The Boy Called Troublemaker

Surfer of the Century: The Life of Duke Kahanamoku

Wind Runner

MORE BOOKS BY SCOTT PETERS

Mystery of the Egyptian Scroll

Mystery of the Egyptian Amulet

Mystery of the Egyptian Temple

Mystery of the Egyptian Mummy

Join the *I Escaped Club* to hear about new releases at:

https://tinyurl.com/escaped-club

BIBLIOGRAPHY

Graves, Mary Ann. "Letter from California." Illinois Gazette (Lacon, IL), September 9, 1847.

Houghton, Eliza Donner, *The Expedition of the Donner Party and its Tragic Fate,* Chicago: A.C. McClurg and Co., 1911

Johnson, Kristin, *Unfortunate Emigrants, Narratives of the Donner Party,* Logan, Utah. Utah State University Press 1996

McGlashan, C.F. *History of the Donner Party: A Tragedy of the Sierra,* Stanford, Calif: University Press 1940

Murphy, Virginia Reed. "Across the Plains in the Donner Party {1846}: A Personal Narrative of the Overland Trip to California." Century Illustrated Magazine42 (July 1891): 409-26.

Reed, James, "The Snow-Bound, Starved Emigrants of 1846." Pacific Rural Press. March 25, April 1, 1871.

Stewart, George R. "Ordeal by Hunger: The Story of the Donner Party." New York: H. Holt, 1936.

https://www.sierracollege.edu/ejournals/jsnhb/v1n1/LKeseberg2.html

DID YOU ENJOY I ESCAPED THE DONNER PARTY?

WOULD YOU...REVIEW?

Online reviews are crucial for emerging authors like us. They help bring credibility and make books more discoverable by new readers. We'd love for you to take a few moments and write a short honest review on Amazon and tell a friend about our books.

Join Our Readers List!
Get an email whenever we release a new book. Sign up now! https://tinyurl.com/escaped-club

Made in United States
North Haven, CT
15 December 2021

12811428R00071